BLUE KNIGHTS

&

WHITE LIES

A Larry Gillam and Sam Lovett Novel

by

WILLIAM N. GILMORE

William N. Gilmore

Second Edition

Book cover design by William N. Gilmore and by Arewa Lanre of Graphic_pro360 (a Fiverr.com© seller)

This is a work of fiction. Names, characters, and incidents are the product of the author's imagination or are used fictitiously, and any resemblance to actual persons, living or dead, businesses, companies, events, or locals are entirely coincidental. Did I tell you this is a work of fiction? It is.

ISBN:978-1-946689-09-2

Printed in the United States of America

BLUE KNIGHTS

&

WHITE LIES

WILLIAM N. GILMORE

Books by
William N. Gilmore

Books in the Larry Gillam and Sam Lovett
Novel Series

Book One: Blue Bloods & Black Hearts

Book Two: Gold Badges & Dark Souls

Caution in the Wind Series

Book One: Partnerships

Book Two: The Treasure Seekers

Book Three: The Rescuers

Other Books

No Space For Justice

Saints, Sinners, Lovers and Others

Poems and Prose

From Thoughts That Arose

To my wife, Esther, and the rest of our wonderful family.

Family is created, not in blood, but with love.

CHAPTER 1

Detective Sergeant Larry Gillam walked into the office of the Narcotics Squad at the Atlanta Police Department. He went straight to his desk. Not the desk which sat in the office he was taking over as the temporary commander of the unit, but his same old desk which sat across from his partner, Sam Lovett.

It was his desk, his chair. All his stuff was still there. He hadn't moved a thing. He sat in the chair which had a cushion on the seat having become formed to his body over the years. It was comfortable. It was safe.

Sam wasn't there yet. Which was typical of Sam on a Monday morning; most mornings, actually. That was something he would have to talk with him about. As the new boss, he couldn't show favoritism. He had to be fair to everyone.

Speaking of everyone, Larry looked around and then at his watch. It was almost ten o'clock in the morning. No one was at their desk. There didn't seem to be any activity going on at all. He didn't remember anything about an early morning raid or any special training. Just because he was new to the position, he didn't want the other detectives to take advantage of his easy demeanor and friendship.

He decided to have a squad meeting when everyone showed up and discuss this along with several other things which needed to be addressed. He didn't want to be a hard ass, but there was still work to do. Crime didn't oversleep or take vacation.

Gillam felt unusually tired. He didn't think he got much sleep last night. All the events of the past couple days weighed heavy on his thoughts. The connection between Lieutenant Jones and Operation Back Street, the shoot-out with Jones, and Jones' swan dive which left him about a foot shorter.

Larry gingerly rubbed the leg Jones shot, but there was no pain and there was no longer a bandage around the wound. He squeezed the leg a little harder and there was no pain at all.

Either the doctors did a great job or the medicine was working wonders.

Funny he didn't notice it while walking into the office. He just thought about it and there didn't even seem to be a limp anymore. He thought about it some more and he couldn't even remember the walk from the parking lot. It must be the medicine. He would have to cut back now that he was back at work.

It was time for everyone to be back at work. This was getting on his nerves that no one had bothered to come in on time. He was getting pretty perturbed. He picked up the phone on his desk and called Sam's cell. It rang several times before he heard an answer.

"Hello," said a rather groggy voice.

"Hello, yourself. What'd you do, turn off your alarm, roll over, and go back to sleep?"

"Larry? Larry, is that you?"

"Yes, it's me. Your new boss. The head hauncho. Get your sorry butt out of bed and get in here before I have to write you up."

"Where are you? Are you okay?" Sam asked, fully awake now and sounding like he was almost in a panic.

"I'm where you should be, at the office. You sound like you were having a bad dream. Good thing I woke you. Now get up, get cleaned up, and get in here. By the way, where is everyone? Is there something going on I missed?"

"You're at the Narcotics office? Don't move. Don't go anywhere. I'll be there as quick as I can. You're sure you're all right?"

"Yes, Sam, my leg is fine."

"Your leg? Oh, yeah, your leg. I'll be there just as quick as I can. Just don't go anywhere."

"You are one strange bird, Lovett. See you in a bit."

CHAPTER 2

Sam Lovett came running into the Narcotics Squad and found Larry sitting at his desk. Behind Sam was his wife, Debbie. Larry wasn't sure which one had the strangest expression on their face; or why.

"Okay," Larry said. "What's going on? Am I being punked or what? Where is everyone?"

Sam stared at him and finally got out, "Where have you been?"

Debbie, her hands to the sides of her face, just gave out an, "Oh, my God!"

"Both of you are starting to scare me." He said, coming out of the chair. "And Debbie, what are you doing here? Sam, don't tell me this is some kind of surprise party or celebration. I'll really get upset. You know I don't like that kind of stuff."

"A party?" Sam repeated, overly loud. "Just tell us where you have been this past week? Everyone's been looking for you. There's a state-wide BOLO out for you. I've been all over the city and county looking for you."

"What are you talking about, Sam." Larry put his hands out. "I've been right here. Well, not here at the office, but, here."

"What's the last thing you remember? What day is this?"

Debbie asked.

"What do you mean? Why all the questions?" Gillam asked, puzzled at the interrogation.

"Humor us," Sam said.

"There's no humor in this," Larry returned, eyes narrowing. He looked at his two friends in bewilderment and shook his head. "All right. I'll play along. It's Monday morning." He looked at his watch. "It's just before eleven a.m. I'm Detective Sergeant Larry Gillam, she's Debbie Lovett, your wife, and you, you are about to be Officer Lovett if you don't start telling me what the hell is going on."

"First of all," Sam started, looking at Debbie in disbelief then back at Gillam. "It's Sunday and it's just now 7:15 in the morning. You were last seen over a week ago. Your rental car was found abandoned on some country road pull-off by the State Patrol with the keys still in it, along with your dead cell phone. When did you get to the office and how?"

Now it was Larry's turn to look at Sam in disbelief. "I got here this morning, about an hour ago. I…, I guess I drove here. I don't seem to remember too clearly. I was at the front entrance and I came inside—

"What about this past week?" Debbie suggested.

"What do you mean this past week? I just talked to Connie the other night. Ask her! We're going up to the North Georgia mountains this weekend. Or was it last weekend? Did we go? Oh, God, did I forget? I stood her up, didn't I?"

"That was last week. Connie's been worried sick about you," Sam said. "We all have. She hasn't heard from you for over a week. She's the one who called us. We thought you were just taking some time off to heal and get over the stress of everything with the Jones incident. After she called us I went over to check your apartment and took care of Cali when we couldn't find you, and there were no notes or messages. I got Bubba to go over and stay with Cali hoping you would show up there, or at least call."

"Is it really Sunday? No wonder no one is here now. I just got my days mixed up. That's all. It must be the medication I'm on. I'm a little hazy about things because of it. I'll be okay in a little bit. I'm tired. Maybe I did come back too soon." He sat heavily back in the chair, letting his unsupported bulk sink into the cushion. He gave a sigh. His eyes seemed to be staring far out into nowhere. He wasn't getting it.

"Larry," Sam began, "do you remember driving your rental car out into the country? Taking some back roads at night? Stopping somewhere?"

"Yeah, I do that all the time, it relaxes me, helps me get my thoughts together. I did that just the other night after talking to Connie. I think I had some car problems though. I…, I don't remember what I did next. Maybe I fell asleep in the car."

"You said you found yourself at the entrance of the office," Debbie said. "Do you remember how you got there? Did someone drop you off? Do you remember anything before that?

Anything at all? Did you do any drinking? Or drugs? Could you have hit your head?"

"No. No. No, and no! I can't remember right now. My head is spinning from all these questions." He shook his head and then put his face into his hands. "I need to lie down. Maybe get some sleep."

"Where's your gun and badge, Larry?" Sam asked.

Larry felt down to his belt where he wore his badge, then to his side; nothing there. He then reached for the billfold holding his other badge and police ID. It wasn't there.

"I don't know. I don't remember if I had it with me when I went for the drive. I should have. I always have it with me." He checked for his ankle-gun. It wasn't there either.

"I think we need to get him to a hospital to get checked out," Debbie told Sam. "Just in case."

"I think you're right," Sam agreed. "I'll call the Chief and advise him, as well as dispatch to call off the BOLO. Why don't you call Connie and have her meet us at the hospital. Maybe seeing her will help him remember something."

Sam finished up his calls while Debbie was still talking to Connie. Larry just sat at his desk with that unfocused stare. Sam went over to him.

"Okay buddy, let's get you up and out to the car. We need to make sure the old you is still in there somewhere." He grabbed Larry's arm and started lifting him up. Larry looked up at him and opened his mouth. The scream that came out startled

Sam so badly, he almost fell backwards, letting go of Larry's arm, dropping him back into the chair. It caused Debbie to jump and give a scream too, dropping her phone.

Larry's scream stopped immediately. He put his arms on the desk and then put his head down on his arms, face down.

"What the hell was that?" Debbie asked. She was shaken, staring at Larry, and backing up just a little, not paying any attention to the far away voice on the phone lying on the floor.

"I just touched him. Getting him ready to go. I don't think I hurt him," Sam said, not wanting to move, not taking his eyes off Gillam.

"Larry? Larry, are you all right?"

Lifting his head, Larry said in a normal, calm voice, "Yeah, sure. You ready to go?"

Debbie looked at Sam, shook her head, and picked up the phone from the floor. She walked away talking softly into it, looking over her shoulder from time to time.

Sam took a step towards Gillam. "Did I hurt you? Are you injured somewhere?"

"What are you talking about? I'm fine."

"You screamed. I thought maybe I had touched a sore spot."

"What do you mean, Sam? I'm just waiting on you, partner. I'm not sore anywhere. Not even my leg hurts anymore. In fact, it's great." He got up from the chair and did a little jig. "See. And I didn't scream. You think I'm a squealing little girl or something? I think you're the one who needs to get checked out. Let's go before I change my mind. Then maybe we can get some work done today."

"It's still Sunday, Larry."

"Are you positive? It sure seems like Monday."

CHAPTER 3

Without another incident, Sam and Debbie got Gillam to their car and on the way to the hospital. Connie was also on her way to meet them there. She had heard the scream and the thud of the phone hitting the floor. When Debbie composed herself enough, she picked the phone up and told her what happened.

Connie was at a loss for words. She hadn't known Larry long, however, through their lengthy telephone conversations and the time they had spent together, she couldn't believe Larry would be having a breakdown or some other mental disorder.

There had to be some other reason for his disappearance and actions. She hoped she would be able to help. She wanted to be with him. Comfort him. And yes, she admitted to herself, love him.

There had been no conversation on the short drive to the hospital. Debbie drove right to the Emergency Room entrance and Sam, sitting in the back with Larry, opened the door and got out. He asked Larry if he wanted him to get a wheelchair or an orderly to help them.

Larry looked at Sam as if he were crazy. "What? You

don't think I can walk, or are you afraid I'll run away?"

"I just want to make things as easy for you as I can, bud. I just thought you might feel better sitting. I don't know how long we're going to have to wait."

"I keep telling you I'm fine. I'll sit when I get inside," he said as he got out of the car.

"I'll find a parking spot," Debbie said. "Then I'll be right in behind you."

"Okay," Sam said. "We'll be right inside checking in. We won't go anywhere without you."

Debbie slowly drove off in search of a parking spot while Sam and Larry entered the Emergency Room. Sam walked beside Larry, cautious not to bump him or make any contact with him, possibly setting off another screaming session. They walked to the check-in desk and Sam pulled his ID out showing it to the lady there.

Sam wasn't sure at first what to say or how to explain why they were there. He thought it best to keep the information to a minimum at this level.

"I'm Detective Lovett and this is my partner, Larry Gillam. He needs to see someone about a situation. He was shot in the leg just over a week ago, but he's had some problems dealing with certain aspects surrounding what happened."

The lady at the desk, Sam wasn't sure if she was a medical professional or an administrator, asked for Larry's medical card.

"I can't seem to find my billfold," Larry said.

"Can you just look it up under his name? Lovett asked. "I'll verify it's him."

She did some typing on the computer and then looked up at Larry and then at Sam.

"Doctor Patel was the doctor who did the surgery on your leg. You're not due for a follow-up until Tuesday. What kind of problems are you having with it?"

Larry looked at the lady with a smile. "None. It feels great. No problems at all."

"That's good," she said. "Then why are you here?"

"Like I said," Sam intervened. "There's some problems we need to speak with a doctor about. There may be some …, ah, emotional problems involved."

"Then you need Mental Health. That's on the eighth floor."

"He needs a full check-up. There may be other injuries we weren't aware of at the time and it's possible his medication is causing some weird side effects. I really think we need to talk with a doctor about it."

Looking at her computer the lady said, "Doctor Menzel was the physician who treated him in the ER when he first came in. He just began his shift. I'll see if I can get you in. It's pretty quiet right now, it should only be about ten to fifteen minutes. We do what we can for our police officers."

"Thank you so much," Sam said.

"Yeah, thanks a bundle," Larry said, smiling again at the lady.

Debbie came in from the parking lot with Connie by her side. "Look who I found outside wandering around," Debbie said.

"Connie!" Larry shouted out and ran over and hugged her. "I'm so sorry I forgot about our date. It must be the medicine I've been taking for my leg. It has me in such a fog."

"Is that what happened to you, Larry?" Connie asked, looking over to Sam for verification. Sam just shrugged his shoulders.

"I don't know. I'm so confused right now. To me it's Monday, but Sam keeps saying it's Sunday of next week, or rather a week from last week. I don't know what it is. What day is it? Maybe you should tell me what year it is too."

It would have been funny if it wasn't so personal. It scared her too.

"Look me in the eyes, Larry," she said, softly and soothingly. "Look at me and try to remember. You called me on a Friday night. We talked a while. A long while. We made plans. And then you must have gone out afterwards. You drove into the country. Something happened. You left the car there. We haven't heard from you until today. It's Sunday. Nine days after we talked. There has been no word from you. No calls. Nothing. What happened to you? Where were you?"

"Nine days?" Larry asked. "How's that possible? I don't

remember much after taking the drive."

He felt his beard. He needed a shave, but it was just a very short stubble. He looked at his clothes. They were in good shape for nine days. They weren't soiled and they didn't smell. He knew Sam liked to kid him and sometimes play tricks on him, but he didn't think Connie would play along with anything this serious.

The way everyone was acting he knew it wasn't a joke. He strained to remember something, anything after the car stalled. Anything before finding himself at the front entrance to the Police Department. It was blank. It wasn't even a fog or a cloud which kept him from seeing anything. It was just..., nothing.

Tears started welling up in his eyes; more from frustration and the confusion than anything else. He took hold of Connie, putting his arms around her, burying his face in her shoulder and neck.

"Everyone must think I'm crazy. Am I?" he asked, choking a little and trying to keep from bursting into sobs.

"No, sweetie, you're not," she said in a whisper, holding him close. "Like you said, it must be the medication. I'm sure of it. It's just causing some side effects which are messing with your head. We'll get it straightened out and you'll be yourself again soon. Then we'll go and do those things we planned. Don't worry. It will be all right. I promise. I won't leave you."

He lifted his head and looked into her eyes and smiled.

"You're wonderful. Thanks for putting up with me. I don't deserve you."

"Detective Gillam," the lady at the check-in desk called to him, "Doctor Menzel is ready to see you now. Go to room seven in the blue zone."

Connie took Larry's hand and they headed towards the examination room. Sam followed and whispered over to Debbie and nodding at the two ahead of them.

"I think that's the best medicine he could have gotten right now."

"I think you're right," Debbie agreed. "It sure looks like they belong together. I hope he's all right."

"I'm sure he is. It's just a combination of all the stress lately and adverse reactions to the medication. It must be like shell shock or what they call post-traumatic stress. What else could it be?"

"You must be right. But where could he have been these past nine days?"

"I don't know. Maybe he'll be able to tell us soon. I sure hope so."

CHAPTER 4

The group was met by a nurse who told Larry to go into the room and change into the hospital gown that was placed on the examining table for him. She directed everyone else to some chairs just down the hallway.

Connie told Larry she would be just outside while he changed and she would come in if he needed her.

He laughed at her a little. Assuring her he would be all right and promised not to run up and down the halls in an open hospital gown.

Doctor Menzel arrived shortly, introducing himself to everyone. Sam remembered him from their previous meeting when Larry was treated following the shooting.

Although Gillam had signed a release of treatment with the ambulance crew at the shooting scene, the Chief of Police had insisted that he be examined at the hospital.

After Lieutenant Jones' body had been removed from the fence, they went to the Emergency Room where Gillam was first treated in the ER by Doctor Menzel. He was then referred to Doctor Patel for the out-patient surgery. Mainly just cleaning and stitching up the wound which would take place that afternoon, and for any follow-up.

It did leave a nice war wound that Larry could show around after he healed. He was also given some strong medications for pain and infection. Apparently, it was a combination of medicines which caused the problems he was having.

Sam told Doctor Menzel what had transpired over the past week and a half, up to finding Larry at the office without any memory and screaming when he grabbed his arm. The doctor showed some concern and told Sam it could have been the medication, but he would give Larry a good work-up and possibly change or take him off the current treatment altogether.

Doctor Menzel entered the examination room. "How you doing, detective," he said, as he pulled back the curtain. He had expected to see Gillam sitting or lying on the table, but he wasn't there. Instead, Gillam was sitting naked in the far corner of the room with his knees up to his chest and his arms around them. He was rocking back and forth; mumbling something incoherent.

The doctor went to the door and called out. "I need a male nurse in here right now."

Sam and Debbie stood up. Connie did as well and took a couple steps forward. The doctor saw her and put his hand up to have her stop.

"Not now," he said. "Everything's all right."

A young man dressed in green scrubs went into the room and the doctor closed the door.

After about ten minutes Doctor Menzel came out. He

closed the door softly behind him. He walked over to the nurse's station and picked up a phone. He was on it for just a couple minutes then walked over to Sam and the others.

"He's doing all right now. He needed to be sedated. He apparently had an anxiety attack while getting changed and now he's resting comfortably."

"Can I see him?" Connie interjected, a world of concern in her voice.

"Not right now," the doctor said. "I still have some things I need to do. Some samples to take and tests to run. I've never seen reactions of this nature to this medication. I'm not sure if that's the problem. It may be more emotional or some other underlying reason, but we'll find out what it is and I'm sure he'll be okay."

"Doctor, I've been Gilliam's partner now for several years. We've been in some really hairy situations and we've had to overcome some pretty stressful things. I know Larry and I know he's stronger than whatever this is."

"Yes, I'm sure he is. May I have a word with you over here?" he asked.

They walked a few feet away. The girls sat and stared, straining to hear.

"You brought him in the day he was shot. How did he act then?"

"He was treated on the scene. He got the wound examined, cleaned, and wrapped up by the ambulance crew and I brought him in a few hours later after we got most of the paperwork done. He hurt some and limped a little, but otherwise he was fine. He was happy to be alive and happy that SOB Jones was finished."

"And he was shot in the left leg?" Doctor Menzel asked.

"You know he was," Sam answered, puzzled. "You treated him."

Just then they were approached by another man in a doctor's frock. He was carrying a large manila envelope. The type used for x-ray films. The cursive stitching over the left pocket of the frock identified him.

"You asked to see me, Doctor Menzel?" The man said, in a strong Indian or Pakistani accent.

"Yes, Doctor Patel. This is Detective Lovett. Detective Gillam's partner. Will you both come with me please." He headed for the examination room and opened the door, allowing the others to enter the examination room ahead of him.

"Thank you, Charles. Would you bring me all the medical files on Detective Gillam," Doctor Menzel asked the male nurse. The nurse exited, closing the door behind him.

Doctor Menzel opened the privacy curtain. Gillam was lying on the table covered with a white sheet up to his chest. He appeared to be sleeping.

"When I first came in, he was sitting up in a fetal position in the corner, rocking. His clothes were folded up neatly in the chair. He was saying something I couldn't understand at first.

We got him up and into a gown, and then onto the table. I believe he was having an anxiety attack and I had the nurse administer a sedative. Once he was calmed, we checked his vitals which were understandably elevated, but not so as to put him in any danger. Then I began checking him closer. I started with the gunshot wound first. Doctor Patel, since you did the surgery, will you please examine the wound."

Doctor Patel approached the table and lifted the sheet above the left leg. He lifted the gown up and began the examination.

Lovett's view was blocked by the doctor and he tried to look around. He still couldn't see anything.

Doctor Patel covered the leg then looked at the right leg. He lowered the sheet and went over to the large x-ray reader on the wall and turned it on. He removed the film from the envelope and put it on the lighted reader. He looked at it a few seconds and then went back over to Gillam and looked again at both legs Again he covered them, then went up and looked Gillam in the face. He turned and looked at Doctor Menzel.

"This is him? You are sure?"

"Yes, doctor, it's him. You know it too."

"What's going on," Lovett inquired. "What's wrong?"

"Is it possible the detective has a twin?" Doctor Patel asked.

"No." Lovett said. "He has no brothers or sisters. What's going on? Why are you asking that?"

"He was shot in the left leg almost two weeks ago," Doctor Menzel said. "I treated him here in the ER. I cleaned the wound. Doctor Patel did the real work of making sure there were no bullet fragments or other internal damages to consider, and he stitched the wound closed. He was due for a follow-up this Tuesday. If he was doing well the stitches may have been removed. Now…, well, take a look yourself."

Lovett went over next to the table Gillam was on and slowly lifted the sheet covering his left leg. He half expected to see Larry's whole leg with stitches like Frankenstein's or an infected ugly slime of gangrene. What he saw was even more surprising.

"Exactly where was he shot, detective?" Doctor Menzel asked.

"Right here," Lovett pointed at a place on Larry's leg. It was a through and through. There was blood all down his leg. There were holes in his pants."

"Where are the injuries to his leg?" Doctor Menzel asked.

"There's not any!" Sam exclaimed. "Why not? Did he have plastic surgery? Is that where he's been?"

"If so, it's the best I've ever seen. It's as if he were never injured," Doctor Patel said. "There is no swelling, no stitches and no sign of any repair."

"How is that possible? I know he was shot there," Sam said, still pointing at a location on Larry's left leg in disbelief. "What about the panic attack? What's causing that?" Sam demanded. "Did you check him for any other injuries? Did you look at his arm? Why would he scream when I grabbed him?"

"I only made a visual examination and there doesn't appear to be any other injuries," Doctor Menzel said. "I'll order additional x-rays and blood work to be sure, but I think it's all in his head right now. The best thing we can do is let him rest.

Maybe we'll get some answers when he wakes up. It may be a few hours yet. I'll have him put in a private room upstairs. You can be with him, but I wouldn't tell them about his leg. Not just yet. It's something we want to look at further."

"Okay, but I don't understand why you don't want them to know about his leg. I'll do as you ask for now, but I want to be the first to know anything. And this is a follow-up from the shooting, so the Department pays for everything; not Gillam. Deal?"

"I think we can live with that," Doctor Menzel said, with a smile.

Sam went out the door to tell the others about Larry being admitted and being moved to a private room.

Doctor Patel turned and faced the intern. "Is there something else you are not telling me, Doctor Menzel?"

"What he was saying while he sat in the corner. I finally made it out. He was saying 'I want to go back.' He kept saying it over and over."

"You mean back to where he was or back home, or work?" Doctor Patel asked.

"I don't think so. The last time he said it, he said he wanted to go back to Earth."

CHAPTER 5

Gillam was in a room on the fourth floor, an isolation section. He was still out from the sedative, but appeared to be resting comfortably. A large window had the first set of sheer drapes pulled closed to allow muted sunlight in.

Connie was by the bed holding Larry's hand and arranged the sheet over him to cover his chest better. Sam and Debbie were just outside the room.

Sam called the Chief to give an update on Larry's condition and that he had been admitted. He held back the part about the leg wound oddity. He wasn't sure it was something he wanted getting out yet. The chief was arranging for an officer to be posted outside the room twenty-four hours a day until Gillam was released.

Doctor Menzel told Sam he would let Gillam rest through the night with constant monitoring, and would order up a battery of tests the nest day as well as consult with someone from the mental health unit and have them check in on him.

They already had taken some blood samples to start their lab work, but it would be a while before they had any results to work with. He suggested they let Gillam rest and come back tomorrow night. Sam agreed and gave the doctor his numbers to reach him in case there was anything else they could do or if there were any other incidents.

Sam and Debbie looked in on Larry one more time and said good night to Connie. They knew she would be there a while.

A uniformed officer arrived just as they were leaving and set up a chair from the waiting room outside Gillam's room. Sam also gave him his contact numbers and instructions that only properly credentialed hospital staff, he and his wife Debbie, as well as Connie were the only ones allowed in the room. A log was to be kept as well as in any controlled security detail. The officer wrote down all the information and assured Lovett he would pass all the instructions to his relief.

Sam and Debbie headed out without much conversation between them until they reached the parking lot. Debbie looked back at the yellow bricked hospital and up to the windows on the fourth floor.

"Do you think he's going to be all right?" she asked somberly.

"Of course, he's going to be all right," he said, putting his arm around his wife. "That's Larry Gillam."

CHAPTER 6

Larry slept quietly. No turning or jerking. No moaning, or facial expressions, or any other things which would show he was dreaming or remembering bad things. Connie was thankful for that. She wanted him to rest comfortably, get well, and get back to his old self. The self that wanted to be with her.

It was now past 11:00 p.m. and she had no intentions to leave Larry that night. She had made a nest in the chair next to his bed. At times, she would take his hand and sometimes even stroke it.

Larry's nurse came in and checked on his progress, administering a mild sedative, per doctor's orders, for him to sleep throughout the night. They felt rest would be the best thing for him right now. More extensive tests would come in the morning. Along with many more questions.

Connie had fallen asleep and was waking to the early morning light coming through the curtain. She looked over at Larry. He wasn't there. She looked over to the bathroom and the door was still open, but no Larry. She went to the door of the room and opened it and saw the uniformed officer standing across from the door.

"Good morning," he said.

"Did they take Larry, ah, Detective Gillam for tests this morning?" Connie asked.

The officer looked at Connie a little strange. "No ma'am. No one has been in or out of the room this morning."

"He's gone," was all that came out. Connie went back in the room followed by the young officer. She went into the bathroom, turned on the light and pulled back the shower curtain. Nothing.

Connie's eyes flew open as she sat up in a panic and the first thing she saw was Larry on the hospital bed, still asleep. She had been dreaming. She took a deep breath, letting the air release slowly. Her heart, still beating at a mile a minute, was just beginning to settle down. She said a little prayer, thankful that it had just been a nightmare.

A knock on the door startled her again for just a second and a nurse opened the door. She carried a tray containing vials and tubes and other instruments and came over to Larry and put the tray on the table beside his bed.

"I need to draw some more blood for tests this morning before breakfast," she told Connie. "He looks so peaceful I almost hate to wake him, but I have to get this done."

"Here, let me," Connie volunteered. She leaned near him as she softly spoke his name and holding his hand. "Larry, Larry darling. The nurse is here to take blood. Larry, it's Connie. Good morning, sleepyhead. Rise and shine."

Larry's eyes fluttered several times then opened. He

blinked and pulled his head back a bit trying to focus, looked at Connie and smiled.

"Hey, you," he said.

"Hey, yourself. Did you sleep well? Feeling better?"

"I think so. I'm still at the hospital, I'm alive, I know my name, but better yet, I know yours."

Connie smiled even bigger. "The nurse is here to draw some blood for your tests today. After that, we'll get you a nice big breakfast."

"Sounds good to me. I'm really hungry for some reason. Eggs, lots of eggs. With bacon and sausage."

"As you said, we are in a hospital. I'm not sure that will fly with them, but I'll see what I can do."

"Ma'am, can you step outside for just a moment while I draw the blood?" The nurse asked. "It's procedure and will just take a minute. Then I'll see about his breakfast."

"Okay," Connie said. "Sweetie, I'll be just outside if you need me." She squeezed his hand. She remembered the first time they met. When they shook hands, he almost didn't let go. This time, she wasn't sure she could.

"Ahem," the nurse gave a little verbal nudge as she looked at Connie.

"Ok," Connie said. "I'll be right back." Giving a wink and one more squeeze to Larry's hand.

The nurse pulled the curtain around the hospital bed as Connie closed the door to the room. She smiled at the officer sitting in the chair.

"How's he doing," the officer asked.

"He slept well and now has a big appetite. I think he's doing much better."

There was a loud clanging as a metal tray hit the floor in the room. They heard Larry yell out, the nurse scream. The officer knocked over his chair as he lunged for the door ahead of Connie. Just as he was opening it, the nurse came running out, almost knocking him down.

"He's sleeping again," Connie told Sam and Debbie, who were listening together on speaker. "The doctor gave him a different, more powerful sedative. Do you think he's going to be all right?" Her voice breaking.

"Yes, of course," Sam said, immediately.

"We're all going to be there for him," Debbie added. "We'll help him through whatever this is. He's family."

"I just don't understand," Connie said. "He woke up and seemed to be himself; then the nurse came and he freaked out again. He was yelling at her; telling her to get away; calling her Grey, and that's not even her name. Who's Grey?"

"I'm not sure," Sam said, slowly. "Is it possible ..., no, forget that. Did he say anything else?"

"No. The doctor did say he would schedule an MRI. I think it's to see if there may have been any brain trauma or something else going on inside."

"If he's sleeping with the medication now," Debbie said, "maybe you should go home, get some rest, and freshen up.

We'll be up there shortly to be with him. Don't wear yourself out. He'll need you strong when he wakes up."

"Yes, that's a good idea. He should be out for at least a few more hours. I'll hurry though."

"No, you get some real rest too. We'll call you if there is any change."

"Okay, but only if you promise to call. You guys are the best. I know Larry thinks so, too."

Connie almost didn't leave, she hated it, but she knew they were right. She need to be strong for Larry, and she would be. She reluctantly headed out of the hospital and home.

It was already late evening when Sam and Debbie finally arrived. The hospital was closed to patient visitations at that hour and there were no other high-profile patients in that special section. It seemed like a ghost town. Sam was allowed special access to his partner's room; day or night.

As they passed the nurses station, Debbie said "Good evening to the lone nurse who was on the phone. The nurse just gave a wave. They were approaching Larry's room and noticed the officer assigned there was not present.

"Could he be inside with Larry, or maybe had to use the

restroom?" Debbie asked.

"There's no reason for him to be in with Larry, unless there was some trouble," Sam said, quickening his pace. "He would have called someone for a relief. The door should never be unmanned."

They got to the room and opened the door. Larry was not in the bed. Sam told Debbie to wait in the room and he went to the nurse's station. When he got there, the nurse was still on the phone.

He waited impatiently for a short time until she put the phone down, covering the mouthpiece, and asked if she could help him. When he inquired about Larry, she said he had been taken to have some tests and the officer insisted on staying with him, wherever he went. Satisfied and relieved, Sam went back to the room to let Debbie know.

"Isn't it a little late for such procedures?" Debbie asked.

"I hope not," Sam replied. "They might still be able to find whatever is effecting him. He's not that far gone."

"No, silly. Late at night. Don't they schedule tests earlier in the day?"

"That's what I was thinking," Sam said, as he looked to the ceiling.

"Of course, you were, my sweet." Debbie said, snickering.

"But I guess they do them when the need arises. Maybe this was the only time he could get them done."

"That's possible, I guess," Debbie agreed. "Something just seems off. I can't put my finger on it."

"I'll go out and ask the nurse how long it might be. If it's going to be a while, we may have to come back tomorrow. I want him to know we were here though, that we didn't abandon him."

"We would never do that and I don't want him even thinking that. I doubt he would. I'll write him a note while you check with the nurse."

Sam went back to the nurse's station, but the nurse was gone. He waited for what seemed ten or more minutes and then started looking up and down the corridors of the ward.

Most doors to the rooms were closed. The quiet and the stillness added to the earie effect of the hospital and unnerved Sam. He started looking all around, especially behind him, stopping at times to see if he could hear someone, anyone.

Not finding the nurse, or any hospital employee, he headed back towards Larry's room. He got back to the nurse's station and looked around that area one more time.

He was about to leave when he heard what sounded like pounding coming from behind one of the doors labeled as a storage room. He tried the door leaver and it opened. He slowly opened the door wider, and saw a pair of feet on the floor. When he fully opened the door, he saw the officer and a young woman on the floor; both were tied and gagged; the woman was wearing only a slip.

He went to the officer first and took the gag out of his mouth.

"What happened?" Lovett demanded, now untying the officer's hands. "Where's Detective Gillam?"

"I don't know," the officer got out hoarsely. He coughed a couple times and tried to talk again. "A nurse went in to check on Detective Gillam and then I felt a sting in my neck and the next thing I knew, I woke up here."

Sam went over to the woman and took her gag out. "What's going on?" Sam asked.

"I'm the night duty nurse," she wheezed. "I guess I was also drugged. Someone from behind stuck a needle in my neck and that's all I remember. I guess they took my clothes."

"Are there any other nurses working in this area," Sam asked.

"No. No one else at all. With only the one patient here, there's no need," the nurse told him.

Sam reached up and took down from a shelf a packaged hospital gown and gave it to the young lady. The officer helped her stand and then turned his back. She tore open the sealed gown and quickly put it on.

"Did either of you see who did this to you?" Sam inquired. "Did she say anything?"

Both shook their heads.

"How are you feeling? Any ill effects?" Sam asked.

Again, they both shook their heads, but the officer tried to say something, cleared his throat several times and tried again.

"How do you know it was a 'she', detective?"

"Because 'she' took the nurse's uniform and only took your gun belt and radio. Plus, I may have seen her at the nurse's station earlier while the two of you were in here." Sam pointed at the officer. "If you can handle it, I want you to get to the phone and call hospital security to shut this place down and then call police dispatch for back-up. We need to secure the hospital, then search this whole place for Gillam if he is even still here."

He turned to the nurse and told her to get a doctor up there to check out both the officer and herself, and if possible, determine what drug was used on them.

Sam rushed back to Gillam's room.

"Took you long enough, old man," Debbie said, then she could tell something was up. "What's wrong?"

"We have a problem."

CHAPTER 7

Gillam was just waking. He had a hard time opening his eyes. It wasn't due to any bright light, there wasn't any. In fact, he was able to get his eyes opened wider and it was as dark as he had ever seen it before.

"I'm blind," he said, out loud.

"You're not blind, you fool," a far-away, female voice said; a voice that seemed familiar.

Larry tried to raise his hands to his face, but they were strapped down.

"What is this?" Larry demanded. "Who are you?"

"Now, that's a fine how-do-you-do," the voice said.

"Brenda?" Larry questioned, not sure if he believed it. "Is that you, Brenda?"

"The one and only," she proclaimed, as she removed a dark bag used as a hood, from Larry's head.

The bright lights caused him to slam shut his eyes until he could first squint, then slowly forcing them open a little wider for a peek to see if it was really her. It was.

"What are you doing here? Why am I strapped to this wheelchair? And why the hood? What—

"Larry, you're in danger."

Lovett met with the hospital security personnel on the first floor at the main entrance. Debbie was with him. He wasn't about to leave her up there alone, unarmed.

While he waited for his police officers, he gave what information he had, which wasn't much, to the hospital security officers. One thing he did know; she was armed, she had a police radio, and she had Larry. Why, was the big question.

He was also asking for any recent surveillance video gone over for anything suspicious; lone females, unknown nurses, or other female employees, Gillam. He hoped he was right about it being a female. A lone female at that. Otherwise, they may be screwed in any kind of search.

"Danger?" Larry, returned. "What do you mean? And again, I ask," he said, with a cock of his head, "why the hood and restraints?"

"You were kind of out of it and I didn't want you to fall out of the chair," Brenda replied, as she removed the straps. "I was moving pretty fast. I put the hood over you in case we ran into someone. I didn't want anyone to recognize you."

"None of this makes any sense," Larry protested as he rubbed his wrists. "Why am I in any danger and what the heck are you doing here, dressed as a nurse?"

"Larry, I'm sorry," Brenda stated, "but I'm the reason you're in danger."

Patrol cars started pulling up to the hospital, blue lights flashing in the night, some just now turning off their sirens. Before long, there were nearly a dozen cars; a few motorcycles too, and more were coming. Even the police helicopter, with its bright spot light and FLIR system, circled above.

Lieutenant Powell got out of one of the cars and started yelling orders to the responders. The entire main building circled. Every entrance was to be covered. Minimal radio traffic unless there was a need. A line of sight between each officer. No one would be allowed to leave and only true emergencies could go in at the Emergency Room entrance.

Lovett came out of the hospital and met with Lieutenant Powell, giving him the latest information he had. Nothing yet on the hospital surveillance cameras, but they were being checked as they spoke. A hospital administrator and the security chief would be helping with the search. They would conduct the search as if it were a live bomb search. Nothing left unturned.

Sam had Debbie retrieve their weapons from their car, but over her protests, he made her promise to stay outside when they conducted the search. Sam was also given a radio by one of the officers.

A platoon of officers would go in and head straight for

the roof. The search would be conducted so as to clear each floor from the top down, hopefully finding them or forcing them down to where other officers would be waiting.

It was going to take some time, and a command center was being set up.

Sam, now armed; Debbie safe; exits manned; and units starting their search from the roof, went back into the hospital. He went straight back to the fourth floor to begin his own search for Gillam. Might as well, he surmised; that's where all this started.

Sam checked Larry's room once more. It would be very embarrassing if he were there. Of course, he wasn't. Sam began looking for any evidence he could find in the room; syringes with the knock-out drug; notes; blood.

He didn't notice anything until he saw some marks on the floor. Marks which were possibly left from the wheels of a heavy-laden wheelchair. A female wouldn't have been able to lift or drag Larry far. She must have used the wheelchair to get him away from the area. Cameras should have caught that, or at least, pick them up somewhere else in the hospital.

Wanting to stay off the radio for now, Sam called Lt. Powell from the nurse's station and gave him an update. The security tapes were still being reviewed, but now they had something more to look for.

"Brenda, I'm still groggy. My brain is still in a fog. What happened?"

"Sorry, Larry, but I had to sedate you. I couldn't chance you calling out or fighting with me."

"You did this?" He shook his head, trying to clear his thoughts. "I must be losing it. I don't understand what's going on. Is this a dream, a nightmare, or a hallucination?"

"I'm afraid it's real. I had to get you out of that room. You were a sitting duck. Now I have to figure a new plan to get you out of this hospital."

"Where's Sam? I need to talk with Sam, he's my partner."

"I know who your partner is, Larry. He's here at the hospital along with his wife and a bunch of your friends looking for you; looking for us. I know everything about you. I even know about that little girlfriend of yours."

"Connie? What's Connie got to do with this?"

"Nothing. Which is the same as anyone else. And let's keep it that way. The less anyone knows, the better they will be."

"But I still don't understand. Talk to me."

"You will. I'll tell you everything. First, I have to get you out of here. Alive if possible."

Sam determined which direction the wheelchair was heading by the faint marks left on the floor. Strange, but they weren't headed for the elevators. The wheelchair wouldn't have been maneuverable up or down the stairs and it was a sure bet, that they were staying away from areas with cameras or hospital personnel.

Sam called Lieutenant Powell. "I don't have any real proof, but I think whoever took Gillam is still on the fourth floor. Can you send me a couple guys to help search?"

"All my units are manning the exits, the exterior of the hospital, or are searching the floors above and below you. We can try to squeeze them in there, but it may take a while. We don't want to miss anything. If I get some additional units available, I'll contact you. For now, I suggest you get back with one of the search teams."

"Okay, lieutenant, thanks," Sam said. He understood Lieutenant Powell's position and the strategy, but Larry was his partner, his friend. With Larry in some kind of danger, he wasn't about to abandon him.

Sam turned off his phone and the radio, just in case. He slowly began to transverse the hallways, checking every door.

An ambulance pulled up to the Emergency Room with red lights flashing. An officer stationed at that entrance watched as the driver, a rather tall and well-built man, wearing overly large blue scrubs, jumped out, going to the back of the ambulance, and opened the rear doors. He began to pull out a gurney with the assistance from another, similarly built and dressed attendant who had been in the back.

On the gurney was a patient, covered in sheets, moaning with apparent pain. The attendants got the gurney down and locked, and began to wheel the patient inside.

"Auto accident," one of the ambulance attendants said to the officer.

The officer gave a nod to them. He didn't have any orders about stopping arrivals at the Emergency Room, just anyone trying to exit.

He watched them as they rounded a corner and out of sight. When they got to an area where they were not seen, the patient, who just happened to be wearing large blue scrubs, jumped off the gurney and handed two of the three silencer equipped submachine guns, which had been hidden under the sheets with him, to the two attendants.

With the submachine guns now hidden under their oversized scrubs, two of the men headed for the elevators while the third would take the stairwell. Their plan was to converge on the fourth floor, eliminating anyone who got in the way of their mission.

Sam was checking every door. If he found one open, he cleared the room quickly and returned to the hallway. He had his weapon at the ready, finger off the trigger though, a safety precaution, just in case he got spooked by something that he shouldn't shoot at; like Gillam.

As he was checking the doors, he saw a light, shinning from under a closed door a little way down. It went out.

Sam slowly made his way to the side of the door. He strained to hear if there was any talking, movement, or other noise coming from the room. It was dead silent.

He crossed over to the door handle side of the door, squatting down; trying to make as small a target as possible. He knew if he opened the door, he would be silhouetted upon entry, making himself very vulnerable. He also knew if Gillam was inside, and was a hostage or a planned target, he might get the first bullet from whoever had him.

He couldn't hesitate. He would have to find, identify, shoot, and get cover if possible, in just about one second of opening the door. And in the dark, no less. A piece of cake.

This is what they signed up for. This is what they trained for. If Gillam survives this, he was thinking, he better put some nice flowers on my grave every week.

Sam, his weapon ready in his right hand, reached up with his left, and took hold of the door handle.

CHAPTER 8

Larry saw Brenda's eyes flick to the door and she started to move.

"Sam," Gillam yelled, quickly. "It's me. Don't shoot. Stand down."

Lovett stopped just before barreling into the room. He let the door handle go and waited. It was Larry's voice all right. He doubted he was being forced to call out. Larry wouldn't do that.

"Are you crazy?" Brenda scolded Gillam. "How do you know that's your partner out there?"

"I know Sam."

"Are you all right, Larry?" Sam yelled, through the door.

"Yes. It's just a misunderstanding. We'll turn the lights on and you can come in."

If this had been anyone else, Sam wouldn't believe them for a second. "Is she in there with you?" Sam asked.

"Yes. She was armed, but she gave me the weapon. We'll explain everything in a minute. You can keep your weapon out as you come in if you want. Just don't shoot anything, especially me."

Sam saw under the door that the lights were turned on again. He believed Larry was now in charge of the situation in the room. They had code words if they were being coerced, or for other dangers, and they were not used.

Sam stood and slowly opened the door, weapon at the ready again, this time with his finger on the trigger. He saw Gillam in a wheelchair holding up a weapon with two fingers. To the side of him, with her hands up, was the woman he saw earlier at the nurse's station on the phone.

Sam quickly scanned the rest of the room and turned back to the pair. "What the Hell is going on?" Lovett demanded.

"I'm sorry to put you through this," Brenda said. "I really didn't have much choice. I just wanted to keep Larry safe."

"Keep him safe?" Sam repeated. "By knocking out a police officer and a nurse, taking her uniform, and getting this whole place shut down? Who are you anyway, lady?"

"Sam, I'm sorry," Gillam said, with a smirk. "Let me introduce you to my ex-wife, Brenda."

CHAPTER 9

Debbie's phone was vibrating. She expected it to be Sam, but it was Connie.

"Hey," Connie said. "I'm trying to get to the hospital, but there's a lot of police activity going on. Do you have any idea what's going on there?"

"Sam and I are here. I'm outside the main entrance. There is a command center set up. Park and I'll meet you there."

"Does this have anything to do with Larry?" She asked, concern in her voice.

The hesitation was a giveaway. "I'll tell you all about it when we meet."

"Tell me Deb, is he okay?"

"I don't know."

Connie came running up to the police command center at the main entrance of the hospital. Debbie saw her and was waving. Before she even got all the way to her, Connie was asking about Larry.

"I just got a call from Sam. Larry's all right. It appears there was a misunderstanding about some things. I'm still not sure what happened, but Larry's fine."

"Was it another episode? Did he try to hurt himself?"

"No sweetie, it wasn't anything like that."

Lieutenant Powell came over to Debbie. "I've heard from Detective Lovett and everything is secure. He's taking Detective Gillam back to his room. I'm going to stick around and get a full report from your husband on what this was all about, but I'm letting all my officers get back to their duties. If nothing else, this was a good training exercise."

"We're waiting for a report ourselves," Debbie said, with a bit of scorn in her voice. "We don't need this kind of excitement."

Debbie and Connie weren't about to wait on Sam to come out, they were going in, headed for the fourth floor.

The three were still in the same room Sam found Larry and Brenda in. He was trying to understand more about the situation and come up with a reason for not arresting Brenda for assault.

He might be able to get the officer to not press charges, especially if he didn't report the officer's gun and radio were taken, but the nurse was something completely different. And he wouldn't blame her either.

"Look," Brenda began, "I know things are a little harry right now, but I assure you, this will all make sense soon."

"How about you give us the Reader's Digest version for now," Sam suggested.

"Larry, I've lied to you about some things, and I kept things from you. I'm a Special Agent with the FBI."

"Since when?" Gillam looked at her, surprised and confused.

"About a year before we were married. I was on a deep cover assignment, but I couldn't tell you. Even after we were married."

Sam chimed in. "You mean—

"Not now, Sam," he said, quickly, not looking away from her, "this is something for me and her to discuss. In private."

The one thing they did agree on for the moment, was to get Larry back to his room and into his bed. With many of the police officers still around, it was hard to worry about his safety.

They started out of the room and into the hallway. As soon as Sam stepped out, a near silent barrage of bullets flew just over his head, striking the walls and door frame. He dove back into the room, knocking Gillam's wheelchair pushed by Brenda, back from the doorway, knocking Brenda down.

"Oh, crap, there here already," Brenda stated.

"Who are they?" Sam asked, as he quickly got up and hugged the wall of the inner door frame.

"Guys with guns." Brenda gave the simple answer. "They're the ones I believe were sent to get Larry. How the Hell did they get up here with all the cops around?"

"I don't know, but I hope they're still around. Larry, call Lieutenant Powell and get some help up here. I'll try to hold them off. How many were you expecting, Brenda?"

"A crew of two to four; well-trained; well-armed."

"A crew?" Sam almost shouted. "You mean professionals? Why?"

"Let's not worry about that right now, Sam, let's worry about getting out of here," Gillam said, getting out of the wheelchair and holding his hand out. "Give me the gun, Brenda."

"Are you sure you're up to this?" She asked.

He gave her a look that didn't need an answer and she handed it over. She removed the two spare magazines from the officer's gun belt and gave one to Larry and the other to Sam.

Sam didn't radio anyone specifically, He just yelled into the radio. "Signal 63, officers on the fourth floor of Grady Hospital. Signal 63. Shots fired, fourth floor."

Lieutenant Powell heard the transmission and quickly recalled all the officers. Once again, sirens and blue lights filled the night.

For some reason, the elevators didn't seem to be working. "It's only the fourth floor, want to take a hike?" Debbie asked, Connie.

"Anything to get up there as quick as we can," she answered. "I just want to make sure Larry's okay. Then I'll be able to relax a bit."

"I wouldn't worry about them now. They're probably in Larry's room, either watching some sports show or sound asleep."

Both women laughed and headed for the stairwell, unaware what was going on four floors above their heads.

Lovett did a quick peek to see the location of the bad guys and almost got a face full of lead. He saw there were two at the end of the hallway, one on either side. He also saw that between them and the shooters, were several large metal cabinets on wheels.

Most were waist high, but one, a few doors down and on their side, was almost as tall as himself. He was able to just see over it and it had provided some cover when the shooting began.

"Larry, I've got an idea," Sam said.

"This doesn't sound good," Gillam replied. "Why don't we wait for the back-up?"

"I think they're getting ready to make a move. We may not have time."

"Fire a couple shots at them. That should make them wait a bit," Brenda said.

"I don't want them to know we're armed," Sam said. "Not yet, anyway. If I can get them to commit to coming down the hallway, we may be able to trap them."

"You do know they have machine guns?" Brenda stated, more than asking.

"We know that, but they don't know we have two handguns," Sam smiled.

Sam quickly explained his plan. Larry didn't like it even a little bit, but gave in, feeling it was the best they were going to be able to pull off.

"By the way, agent, where's your gun?" Sam asked

"I left it in my car. It would have been hard to explain."

They had Brenda take cover in the back of the room.

The girls stopped on the third-floor landing to catch their breath.

"I knew I should have worked more on that stair-stepper," Debbie said, breathing deeply.

"Not far now," Connie returned, ready to get there.

Smiling, she said, "I like to walk the trails at Stone Mountain and up in Blue Ridge. Helps keep me in shape."

"I'll be in shape soon," Debbie stated. "Round's a shape, right?"

"That's funny," Connie said. "You're in …, wait …, what?"

Debbie just stared at her and gave her a grin.

"How far?"

"Just a couple of weeks."

"Oh, that's wonderful," Connie said, grabbing her and giving her a big hug. "Of course, Sam knows, you've told him?"

"I wanted to get it confirmed first. I was going to tell him tonight when we got home. Just the two of us."

"You mean the three of you. He'll be so thrilled. Congratulations. You'll make wonderful parents."

"Thanks. Let's get going again. Just one more to go."

Sam crouched down and took off for the metal cabinet, getting there just as bullets ricocheted off the far side of it. He was glad they weren't using armor piercing rounds. He grabbed the handle on his side and began to back up with it, heading towards the room he just came from.

The two bad guys came from their cover location firing a burst in Sam's direction as they continued down the hallway.

As they did, Larry leaned out of the doorway, firing at the one on the left, dropping him with two shots. The second guy, startled at the sudden and unexpected, noisy attack, hesitated for a split second too long in bringing the submachine gun up to fire at Gillam. Sam popped around the right side of the cabinet on one knee, shooting the big man several times, dropping him in his tracks.

Both bad guys were down and out. As Sam and Larry, looked down at them, they didn't see their comrade who had emerged from the far stairwell into the hallway and take aim at them.

Two loud blasts made them jump. They turned, ready to return fire as they expected to see another. They did. The machine gun that had been aimed at them, fell to the floor just before he did. The third bad guy was erased. Debbie stood in the hospital hallway with her gun still aimed at the place he once stood. Connie, cowered behind Debbie, her hands over her mouth, eyes wide.

Debbie slowly lowered the gun and took a few steps forward. She stared at the body on the floor for a few seconds as Sam and Larry looked on in disbelief. Debbie kicked the unfeeling corpse, yelling at it, "That will teach you to mess with an armed, pregnant woman's man, you bastard."

Sam rushed over to Debbie and took the gun from her surprisingly steady hand. He looked at her for a moment and smiled, then she hugged him, and started to sob.

Larry went over to Connie and put his arms around her.

She began to cry as well.

"Why are you crying?" he softly asked. "It just seems the right thing to do."

Brenda peeked out of the room and seeing the situation, walked into the hallway. Questioning eyes suddenly turning on her as she asked, "What'd I miss?"

Lieutenant Powell and numerous officers entered the hallway from the stairwell. They handcuffed the assailants before confirming all three were dead. During a sweep of the floor, an unarmed officer and a young lady in a hospital gown were discovered hiding in a storage room. A complete search of the hospital would now be made.

William N. Gilmore

CHAPTER 10

Lovett and Gillam quickly spoke with the officer and the nurse, who was now back in her uniform, before he gave a report to Lieutenant Powell about the assault. Debbie and Connie were giving statements. As was the procedure, Debbie had to surrender her gun for now for the investigation and ballistics.

Gillam and Lovett did as well, with Gillam explaining he was holding the officer's gun belt with his weapon and radio while the officer, who became sick with no time to call for relief, was in the restroom, when everything went down. It had turned out to be a good thing though, helping to save their lives.

The nurse told the lieutenant she had given her uniform to the FBI Agent to help her in her undercover investigation before the arrival of the assault team. She was then told to hide in the supply room.

At least, that's the report that was being made. The young officer was more than happy to corroborate the detective's report, and the nurse, agreeing to cooperate after Lovett told her it might not look good for her career, being only half dressed along with a strange man, in the supply closet.

Brenda, having slipped back into her recovered street clothes, just stood to the side, not talking with anyone. While everyone was engaged, she quietly slipped out and went down the other stairwell.

For the time being, there were few answers given by Gillam and Lovett about the female FBI Agent and what she knew and how she knew it. To be honest, they really didn't have any answers either.

Several doctors and attendants arrived when the floor and the rest of the hospital were cleared. They got Gillam back to his room and after a quick examination, allowed Lovett, Debbie, and Connie back in.

Once they were alone, Lovett voiced his concerns, "We still have a problem. These guys were after Larry. If I hadn't been here, things may have turned out different. It's possible—

Debbie gave him a slap on the back of the head. "Duh, you think? And where would you have been if I hadn't been here?"

"Sorry," Sam said. "I mean, if we hadn't been here. Thanks honey, for saving our butts."

"Oh, yes, thanks," Larry said, as he adjusted the bed to a sitting up position, "but let's get back to the really important thing right now. Deb, you're pregnant?"

She looked at Sam. "I'm sorry you had to find out this way, sweetie. I just got the confirmation today and was going to tell you tonight, but then all this happened." A tear was forming in one of her eyes again.

Sam smiled, bringing up his hands to hold her face and used a thumb to wipe away the tear. "Nothing else matters right now, other than you and the baby are safe. You've made me the happiest man on Earth."

Connie was about to say something, but was stopped by Larry's moaning. He was trying to speak. They all stared at him, his eyes were wide, unfocused, a complete blank expression. He said something again. It sounded like "Earth."

"Sam, call for the doctor," Debbie said, quickly.

Sam reached for the call button and Larry grabbed his arm, not looking at him.

"No," Larry said, surprising everyone. "Wait."

Everyone was quiet, staring at Larry, waiting to see what happened next.

Gillam blinked a couple of times, closed his eyes for a moment and shook his head before opening them again. His focus was back as he looked around the room. He turned to Sam, then to the girls, and then back to Sam. He released Sam's arm. "I'm okay. I am. I just needed a moment to understand what was going on. I think I'm starting to remember some things."

William N. Gilmore

CHAPTER 11

Lieutenant Powell came into Gillam's room. "I've got the feed from the security cameras," he said, holding up a notebook device for them to see. "It shows the three men coming into the hospital from the Emergency Room entrance. They came in an ambulance. We're still checking on that, but it appears it was stolen. One was under a sheet on a gurney as a decoy brought in by the other two. Just after they entered, two of them took the elevator and the one under the sheet went to the stairway."

"Do you have any identification on them yet?" Lovett asked.

"No," Lieutenant Powell said, "and that's the funny part. There's nothing, and I mean absolutely nothing, on them." "We've seen this before," Lovett said, shaking his head.

"Is the Medical Examiner on scene yet?"

"Yes, he and his assistant, a huge guy with a big smile, arrived not long ago. They said they would drop in on you when they got through. I didn't know what he meant at the time, but after he made a quick examination of the attackers, he used the portable digital fingerprint reader on each one and said something funny."

"What was that?" Gillam asked.

"He said something to the effect, 'Here we go again'. He told me a fingerprint check came back with no information on any of the three. They didn't have any identification on them, and nothing in their pockets, except the one who went into the stairwell; he had the keys to the ambulance. The weapons, which were all H&K MP7's, specially equipped with military-grade silencers, didn't have serial numbers or any markings which we could distinguish, but they will be closely checked by ballistics."

"Are you saying the serial numbers had been removed?" Gillam asked.

"I don't think so. I'm not an expert," Lieutenant Powell added, "but it looks like there never were any. The cartridges, a very unique kind, also were unmarked."

"Someone sent those guys after Larry," Sam said. "Someone with resources and determination, whatever the motive might be. We need to find out who those guys are fast and why. It's obvious he's not safe here. That was too bold of an attack. There might be more. We need to get him out of here and to a safe-house. Not just for him, but to keep everyone in the hospital safe."

"There's more," Lieutenant Powell said. "The so-called FBI Agent. She came in about a half hour before the assault team. We have her on camera on the first floor, but shortly after that is when the feed was lost for the fourth floor. We have her leaving before being questioned. Are we sure she is an FBI Agent and not an advance for the assault team?"

"She wasn't with those guys," Gillam said, emphatically. "She came here to warn me and she tried to get me out before they arrived."

"That's just it," the lieutenant continued. "Who is she and how did she know about the assault? Why didn't she notify anyone else? And why didn't she stick around?"

"I don't have all the answers to that," Gillam said. "But she saved my life." He didn't go into their relationship.

"We can hang around and wait for there to be another attack," Debbie finally chimed up, "or we can get Larry out of here and then try to get answers as we can."

Connie, who had been standing back, nodded her head without uttering a word.

"What about his, ah …, medical condition?" Powell asked, looking at Lovett; not wanting to say something insensitive.

"I think I'm going to be fine, lieutenant. I think I know what was causing my reactions and I believe I've taken control of it." Gillam stated.

"Where would you go and how are you going to get there?" Lieutenant Powell enquired.

"I think the least information getting out would be best," Lovett said. "As for getting there, toss me those keys."

"What can we do to help?" Doctor Higdon asked, as he and Mutumbo entered the room.

CHAPTER 12

The Sun was just coming up. Birds were singing, flowers were opening, and bees buzzed around. It looked like it was going to be a nice day.

Well, maybe not so much for those who were in the four large, black, body-bags. Doctor Higdon and Mutumbo placed them into the Medical Examiner's wagon for transport to their office.

It was going to be a very busy day for the pair as they would try to identify the men who made the assault on the hospital, as well as perform the autopsies, and write the reports.

An initial check was made of the stolen ambulance by several CSI personnel. A wrecker arrived for it to be taken to impound where another CSI unit could go over it more thoroughly and try to find evidence connecting it to the assailants. The back doors were closed and the wrecker lifted the front of it up, securing it before taking off.

Sam, Debbie, and Connie were taken to another section area of the hospital. They were placed in the back of a maintenance vehicle and driven away.

The large police presence at the hospital started to dwindle and just a few cars remained, including some of the investigative units and forensics. Their job was going to take a while longer.

Two sets of eyes, one using binoculars, watched from afar in a non-descript van with tinted windows. The mission was in jeopardy. From what they could tell, their comrades had failed. All three, somehow taken out of action; which was in itself, remarkable. As such, they would not be able to be questioned, and therefore, not a liability. The target though, apparently survived the initial assault. That was a problem.

They knew they would have to complete the mission, even if they ended up like the rest of their team. They would not be able to return without results. There was too much at stake.

A cell-phone buzzed and one of the men answered it. Information was passed and instructions were received. No questions were asked on what they were to do next. He ended the call and took out the SIM card, destroying it. He then rolled down the passenger window and waited.

After about thirty minutes, a person on a bicycle went by the van, tossing a plain, brown-paper bag into the open window.

Dr. Higdon and Mutumbo arrived at the ME's office and unloaded the four body bags, taking them straight into one of the examining rooms.

"I'll start on the first one," Dr. Higdon told Mutumbo, "if you would be so kind as to set up the second."

"It be my pleasure, doctor," Mutumbo said, with a big smile.

Two men dressed as doctors, complete with stethoscopes around their necks and authentic identification badges on their white coats, were stopped as they entered the hospital at the employee's entrance. There was a security checkpoint at the entrance and it was manned by three Atlanta Police Officers instead of the regular hospital security. One officer took the identification badges and ran them through a scanner that had red and green indicators.

The first card was swiped through the scanner and the light turned green. The young officer smiled as he handed it back to the doctor.

The second was put through it, but there was a pause of a few seconds. One of the officers in the background cautiously put his blue-gloved hand on his service weapon, but after a short wait, the scanner turned green again. The officer relaxed, putting his hand by his side.

The two men, were instructed to empty their pockets and place the contents and the stethoscopes into a plastic bin, then one at a time, take their shoes off and walk through a metal detector like the ones at airports. Both did so and the detector remained silent. A complete body frisk was then made by the glove wearing officer, as well as an inspection of the shoes and other items in the bin.

Passing all the tests, the doctors were returned all their items and allowed to continue. They went through double doors and into the main hospital.

Shortly after going through the doors, one of the doctors looked at the other, smiled and said, "Guns aren't always needed. Hospitals are full of wonderful things, even deadly things."

"And the police think we are idiots and can fall for their stupid tricks," the other said.

The fourth-floor elevators opened and two bogus doctors stepped out. They walked to the nurse's station where a pretty nurse sat behind the desk. An officer was standing to the side.

"Hi," one of the doctors began. "We're here to take Detective Gillam for his MRI." He showed his identification to the officer and the nurse. "Is he ready?" He looked down the hallway and saw two more officers sitting outside a room.

"Oh, I'm sorry," the nurse said. "With everything going on, I didn't think he would still be going."

"We still have to get all the tests run, it will take a while to get the results in. We'd rather not have to come back."

"Oh, he's just resting. I think it will be all right. He'll need an escort though. Check with the officers at the room."

The pretend doctors walked down to the room and again, they showed their identification. "We need to take Detective Gillam for an MRI. I understand we need an escort."

"That's correct," one officer said. "We can't leave our

post here, so I'll radio you one."

"Great," said the doctor. "Can we get him ready while we wait? It would save us some time."

"He's been sleeping pretty hard. May take a bit to wake him, but go ahead."

The doctors entered the room, closing the door behind them. One pulled a large syringe from the pocket of his lab coat, holding it up, ready to strike. The other pulled the privacy curtain back.

Half a dozen gun barrels were pointed in their direction, and behind them, the door opened. There were two officers, and a very pretty, make-believe nurse with a very real shotgun, ready to unload on them if they tried anything.

The imposters had nowhere to go. The phony doctor with the syringe lowered his arm quickly and plunged the needle into his own thigh. Almost immediately, he fell to the floor and began to shake. The shaking quickly stopped and the man made no more movement. He had taken the easy way out. His partner, who was quickly handcuffed, would not be so lucky.

Bubba Thomson drove through the front gate and waved at the new twenty-four-hour security he had in place there. The gate would be shut and locked during the evening, with a guard checking everyone in and out during business hours.

After Granger's autopsy, Bubba had learned the truth

from Doris about how he had died. The killer's identity was unknown and Bubba believed he may still be on the loose. Bubba was taking no chances that someone would come after him.

He pulled the ambulance around to the back side of the main office building at the impound yard he now owned, and lowered it there. He went to the back of the ambulance and opened the doors. Out stepped Gillam, wearing a CSI jacket and low fitting CSI hat.

"Where is she?" Gillam asked, removing the hat. "She's up front," Bubba answered.

Gillam went to the wrecker and opened the passenger door. Cali jumped into his arms, rubbing her head on his chin and cheeks, purring loudly. "I've missed you too, girl."

CHAPTER 13

Brenda marched into the headquarters of the Atlanta Police Department, quickly flashing a badge and FBI identification, demanding to speak with whomever oversaw the investigation of the debacle at Grady Hospital.

The officer at the front desk quickly got on the phone and asked for someone from the Homicide Squad to come down and meet with the FBI Agent.

Detective John Starling came down and introduced himself to the young lady making demands. "How may we help you?"

"I'd like to have access to the prisoner from the assault at the hospital," Brenda stated.

"That's not going to be possible right now, Agent ...,

"Gillam," she threw out. "And why, may I ask, is the reason I can't question him now?"

"Don't you know?" Starling asked, staring at her.

"I only know that if you don't allow me to question him right now, you could be charged with felony obstruction of a federal officer."

"I doubt that very seriously, Agent Gillam. You see, he's been transported to the FBI headquarters for further investigation."

"Oh," was all she said, before turning and hurriedly heading for the exit.

Doctor Higdon and Mutumbo were near completion with the bodies from the hospital assault; all three of them. The fourth body-bag had been emptied of all the sheets and items it was stuffed with. It had been too obvious that it did not contain a body.

None of the three had anything which would lead to an identification. There were no tattoos or brands, yet they each had scars and evidence of previous broken bones, stab wounds, gunshot wounds, and one even had previous shrapnel wounds with some shrapnel still in his body. The information led them to believe they may have some military background or connection.

Doctor Higdon couldn't even confirm, for now, their country of origin; however, he did have an idea and would do more testing. There were ways to get to the information and it would be an excellent learning experience for Mutumbo.

Gillam entered the office through a back door. Inside sat Sam, Debbie, and Connie. They all stood at once. Connie rushed over and as soon as he placed Cali on the floor, put her arms around Larry. "I'm so glad you're okay. You are okay, aren't you?"

"Better than I've been in weeks," Larry said. He turned to Sam. "How'd everything work out?"

"Just about the way we planned," Lovett smiled. "We made sure no one followed us from the hospital and arranged a car switch under a large underpass just to make sure. We picked up Connie in another underpass and came here through back streets, again making sure we weren't followed.

"I believe that was a good idea, just in case there was any kind of aerial surveillance," Gillam stated. "I don't know how far their reach is. They could even have use of satellites."

"Just as long as it's not those damn UFO's," Lovett emphasized. "As you can see, the diversion we set up with Doctor Higdon allowed you to stay in the ambulance and get away from the hospital unseen. It was easy to tell the form in the fourth body-bag was not a real body. We didn't want them believing it was and going after the doctor. We got them to believe you were still in the hospital."

"Was it another three-man team?" Larry asked. "We're they armed?"

"No, it was only two, both were unarmed, but one of them gave himself a lethal dose of morphine that was meant for you. We have the other in custody. No ID yet. He's not being too cooperative."

"Let me have a crack at him, he'll talk," Larry said, irritably. "Was there anything else about them?"

"It's pretty much like the three from earlier," Sam stated. "There's nothing on them. Doctor Higdon is working on it and will let us know what he comes up with. We've got a van the two were surveilling us from, it's being held as evidence over at HQ. Not much there either, but we're still checking. Our guys did a great job.

"Sounds great. Is there a problem?" Larry asked, concerned.

"We need to talk. In private."

CHAPTER 14

Doctor Higdon and Mutumbo took samples of blood, hair, nails, and stomach contents for analysis. Doctor Higdon sent some of the samples to the Georgia State Crime Lab at the GBI and the rest would be for their own tests.

Although his office was well equipped, he didn't have a DNA Sequencer. He couldn't justify the cost in his budget and the budgets had been sliced to the bones. Instead of getting results in hours, they may have to wait days to get the results from the Crime Lab.

One thing that he did have in his lab though was a mass spectrometer. Doctor Higdon was old school. His background in forensic anthropology would be of great help. He showed Mutumbo how to run the hair sample through the machine.

"Everything you eat or drink," Doctor Higdon began, "and even the air you breathe, leaves its signature behind, and it can last for many weeks or sometimes years depending on the length of the hair. It can tell us where someone has been and even how long they were there.

"What if they do not have hair?" Mutumbo asked, running his large hand over his smooth head.

"The hair can come from anywhere on the body," Doctor

Higdon advised. "Hair grows about 9 to 11mm per month. The machine reads the isotopes or the atomic weight of the elements in the hair. The results are listed on a stick diagram to show which and how much of the elements are present. By using known variables from samples gathered all over the Earth, you can find the location which matches closest to the readout."

"Then you will soon tell where these bad men who tried to kill our friend, Detective Larry Gillam, came from?" Mutumbo asked.

"Yes," Doctor Higdon said, smiling at first, then becoming very serious. "But that will not tell us who sent them or why."

Larry and Sam went into another office where they could talk.

"Okay, Sam," Larry said. "what's up? Did I do something out of character again, or something wrong during the assault?"

"No, you were great. First, I just wanted to check with you. Are you okay? I mean, we were in a shootout. With guys with machine guns. We were fighting for our lives. We—

"Yes, Sam. I'm okay. I'm sorry. I should have checked on you too. It's a very emotional and dark thing to shoot someone. To kill someone. But we killed guys who were trying to kill us. I'd much rather for us to be talking about this than them."

"That was my first," Sam said. "I'm okay with it too. I just hope it's my last, but I can handle it. It won't be a problem."

"I never thought it would," Larry said. "It was my first too. You can't really count Jones."

"It was Debbie's first too. She should never have had a first, but thank goodness she was there, or …, well, you know."

"And in her condition too. Congratulations, by the way. Not exactly the best way to find out, but it sure beats getting a test wand shoved in your face and someone saying, 'This is your fault.' or, 'I'm not sure it's yours.' But I'm happy for you."

"So, true, thanks. How's Connie taking everything?"

"She's a little rattled. I don't blame her. I wouldn't blame her to run off screaming and never call me again."

"I don't think she would do that," Sam said, shaking his head. "She's a real trooper. And it's easy to see how much she cares about you already."

"I'm not sure how I'm going to explain Brenda. I'm not even sure I understand what's going on with her. With us. The whole FBI thing and all."

"That's another thing I wanted to talk about. I got a call just before you arrived. It's about Brenda."

"Is she okay? Did she get hurt?" Larry asked, concerned.

"No. Not that I am aware of, but I'm not sure she's okay. Detective Starling called me. She showed up at HQ asking about the one who was captured."

"And the problem with that?"

"He called his friend at the FBI, Special Agent McGill. You remember him? Well, anyway, Starling asked him about her, and well…,"

"Out with it, Sam."

"She's not with the FBI. Now, or ever."

Gillam hesitated a second. "That could be because her records are deleted," Larry stated. "She's worked deep undercover before. That's what she told me. You know how that works. She may be doing that now. She had knowledge those guys were after me. She saved my life. Why would she lie?"

"I don't know, Larry. But I think it's important to find out why and what she knows."

"But you're still going on the assumption that she's lying. What if she's not?"

"Then we deal with it when we see her again, but if she is, what's her motive? And, is she dangerous?"

"All right, Sam. We'll figure it all out. For now, though, what do I tell Connie?"

"See, she's already dangerous."

CHAPTER 15

Doctor Higdon collected the initial results of his tests on the first three bodies from the hospital assault. He would conduct the fourth later, but was sure the results would be the same.

All three showed they most likely came from an Eastern European country such as Croatia or Syria. He might be able to pin it down more when the DNA results were available.

They may have been part of the wars or conflicts from the countries in those regions and turned into mercenaries, going freelance for the highest pay.

The attack on Gillam obviously was not political or military. He doubted there would be ICE records on them entering the country. They probably would have been smuggled to the U.S. on a large ship, either as part of the crew or as part of the cargo.

CHAPTER 16

Larry and Sam went in with the others. Bubba was holding a sack open.

"You need to give me all your cell phones and electronic stuff," Bubba said.

"What are you talking about," Sam asked.

"We don't want anyone tracking you here."

"He's right, good thinking, Bubba," Larry said, but we need to take out the batteries."

"You can if you want," Bubba said, but I was going to stick them in the microwave. That should keep them from be traced."

"Yeah, I think that would do it," Sam agreed, "but, I think it would be simpler just to take out the batteries. Then you could still use your microwave."

"Okay, then. Take out the batteries and put them in the bag. Now," Bubba insisted. "I don't know if they are tracking you now or not. I don't want them coming around here." Don't use the land line here, that could be tapped.

"What about the ambulance. It's sure to have a GPS in it and how about the car you came in Sam?" Larry asked.

"The car we changed to," Sam said, "doesn't have GPS, and as for the ambulance, it's supposed to be here. If we disconnected it, then that would be a tell-tale sign for anyone who checked.

"I don't know how long we are going to have to be here," Larry said, "but we're going to need some things. Bubba, you're going to have to go do the shopping this time. I'll make you a list."

"I might need to go with him," Larry said. "There's things I need to take a chance to get at my house. Weapons and ammo, the most important."

"Wait until dark," Gillam said. "It might be safer if you were to take an unknown car by yourself, one Bubba could fix you up in, park in the area of your house, and sneak in. Just in case someone is watching. It will also make it harder to follow you as well."

"Good idea," Sam agreed.

"Are you bringing Stella back?"

Sam pointed up. "Are there aliens out there?"

"You bet," Larry laughed.

It was about half an hour before the Sun went down. Larry collected cash from everyone to make sure he had enough for what was needed. After checking around, he made out a list for Bubba, that included a couple of 'burner phones', food, dog and cat food, and toilet paper. He was hoping their stay at the impound lot would not last more than another day or two. If so, they would need to reevaluate their position.

Larry went and sat next to Connie on the new couch Bubba had bought to replace the ugly one Granger had died on. This one was a pretty, blue one which Doris picked out.

"I need to talk to you and tell you about what's going on," Larry said. "Well, not all of it, I mean, about Brenda."

"Okay," was all she said.

"We were married a long time ago. It was very short. Only 20 days. We didn't even go on a honeymoon. I was young, she was pretty, and we both were lonely. Not a good reason to get married, but we drove up to Ringgold on Valentine's day and had a Justice of the Peace do it. We had to have his wife as the witness. It cost us a whole forty dollars. Thirty for him and ten for her. I didn't even have a ring."

"Unprepared as usual," she laughed.

"One night, she called me, and said she couldn't do this anymore, and she was gone. This was the first time I had seen her since."

"She didn't give a reason, and you didn't go after her?" Connie asked.

She didn't tell me why, and I didn't know where she might have gone. I didn't have a clue. She vanished."

"She didn't want to be found," Connie said, shaking her

head. "She was a fool."

"Now, she shows up claiming to be an FBI Agent. Was one when we got married. Saying she's the reason I'm in danger. I don't know what to think."

"She's the reason you're alive now. She knew those men were coming after you. How did she know?"

"I don't know. I don't know how she's involved. Sam says he received information she's not really an FBI Agent. I don't care who she is, I need to get to the bottom of all of this. Make it safe for us all to go home and not to have to keep looking behind us."

"You will," Connie said, squeezing his hand, "I have faith in you."

CHAPTER 17

It was now dark and Sam left out of the impound lot first in an old, dark-colored car that Bubba brought up from the impound yard. It had been towed in from a DUI arrest. It was gassed up and seemed to be sound.

Not too much behind, Bubba left and headed for a large store, somewhere out of the immediate area, to fill the list Gillam had made. He had the guard close and lock the gate. No one, except their own tow trucks already out on runs, was to get back into the lot. Gillam would be in charge until he returned.

Lovett drove around the block of his house and didn't see anything too suspicious. He stopped a half block away on the back street and made his way to the back of his house, having to climb over the fence.

As soon as he was over the fence, he was attacked. It wasn't a vicious attack, it was a loving attack. Stella couldn't be fooled. She knew it was him. She thought it was a game.

"Good girl, Stella. Quiet, now. Good girl."

Stella was a good girl. She wasn't one of those dogs that barked at just anything, she was well trained.

Sam made his way to the back door, trying his best to avoid the automatic security lights, but he had made the angles too good. They popped on just as he got to the door.

He hurriedly unlocked the door and he and Stella got inside. He quickly hit the wall switch for the outside lights and they immediately went out.

Inside the house, there were several lights on that gave him enough light to get through the house without turning anything else on. He went upstairs and Stella followed.

Sam went to his closet, opening the secret door, turning on a light, and began to load into a bag several weapons and boxes of ammo for each. He had an MP5 with several pre-loaded magazines, shot guns, handguns, and several items which may not have been on the approved list of the ATF.

He came out of the closet and was going to Debbie's when he saw Stella, standing rock still, looking at the open bedroom door, and voicing a low growl. He touched her hind quarter and the growling stopped. He gave her a hand signal and she went to the far side of the room, but still alert.

Sam went back to his closet, turning on the light of his hidden room, only partially closing the door. He grabbed his bag, removing a weapon from it as he went across the room. He picked up one of Stella's toys and tossed it towards his open closet door before taking a prone position just inside Debbie's closet, signaling Stella to get in the closet with him. He waited.

CHAPTER 18

The FBI and Homeland Security were attempting to question the only known surviving suspect of the assault. With the information from Dr. Higdon, they brought in a couple of translators to help. They were on either side of the room and repeated the questions of the interrogator.

He still wasn't saying anything. He didn't even ask for an attorney, food, or water. He wore an orange jumpsuit with a belly chain, and his hands and feet were cuffed. He sat at a table, that was bolted to the floor, as straight as he could. A cold, glistening, bottle of water was just out of his reach.

He made no comments or objections to being hooked up to a polygraph machine. It wasn't to see if he was lying or not. While questioning him, the interrogator would hold up pictures to see if there would be any response on the machine.

He first held up pictures of the President, the White House, other government sites just to see if there could be any connection. There didn't appear to be any.

He held up pictures of the other assailants, taken at the ME's office as their bodies lay on autopsy tables, and there was a marginal response. The same occurred when they held up a picture of the hospital. He held up a picture of Gillam, and there was a little more noticeable response. The response was significant though, when he held up a picture of Lovett.

"Lovett was the primary target," one of the interrogators stated, surprised. "Why?"

The suspect never answered, he just gave a slight grin. The stupid FED didn't have all the answers. He continued to look at his reflection in the large mirror that was obviously two-way in the overly warm and bright interrogation room.

The interrogator didn't have all the answers, but he had the suspect, and he was a professional at what he did. He would get answers.

"Your buddies died for nothing. Your mission was a failure. He's alive and you're captured. You're a failure. You obviously weren't trained very well, and your intelligence sucks."

In turn, the translators repeated each question or comment, word for word.

That hit a nerve with the suspect, causing him to grit his teeth and pull on the restraining chains. He cut his eyes to one translator, and just as quickly, straight ahead. The lie detector needle was doing double time. The suspect was sweating and noticeably irritated.

They appeared to be lucky in that the survivor was possibly the weakest link. The interrogator now knew just where to probe.

"Whoever hired you didn't get their money's worth. You

didn't even have the courage of your buddy to kill yourself." The interrogator got down and into his face "It proves you're weak. You're not a professional, you're just a low-life, two-bit crook, trying to make a buck. You can't be any good, you've been fooled, and you're sure not fit to be any kind of a soldier."

Before either translator repeated the interrogator's remarks, the suspect cut his eyes once more, but this time to the interrogator.

"I am more soldier than any of your pathetic Marines," the suspect growled, with a thick accent, once again struggling with the restraints. He gave a sneer towards the interrogator.

With that one short sentence, much was learned about the suspect. They would no longer need the interpreters, he was military or had a military background, His country of origin was narrowed down, and they could get to him.

Behind the two-way mirror, there were smiles, but still concerns about future attacks. Why were they targeting Detective Lovett and Detective Gillam? Who had sent them; who was that woman claiming to be an FBI Agent; and where was Detective Gillam and Lovett now, anyway?

CHAPTER 19

Lovett slowed his breathing, listening, waiting. He had covered himself and his MP5 with some sheets and other items from Debbie's closet. He just hoped they didn't have infrared targeting. Who were these guys?

Slight squeaks from the boards on one of the middle steps. He knew his house. Two squeaks, to be precise. Two coming up the stairs. He didn't know how many more were below or outside though. He waited.

He sensed one at the door of the bedroom. He didn't see him, he just knew he was there. He could hear one of them checking the guest bedroom. Theirs would be next. He prepared himself. He waited.

Sam hoped the light from his closet would draw their attention. He was right. Both entered the bedroom and one of them, not looking down, stepped on Stella's toy, sending out a large squeak from the toy. The startled men were distracted and gave Sam the advantage when he rolled out of Debbie's closet and put both of them down with two quick and quiet burst from his silenced MP5.

Sam quickly changed position just in case there were more on his level he didn't hear. He had been correct in his belief that they were using night-vision goggles. He took one off one of the dead men and put it on his own head and then took the other and placed it in his bag.

The men had been wearing bulletproof vests, but Sam had his own supply of special bullets to get around that. He preferred not to make head shots; the mess would be hard to clean up. He knew Debbie would make him do it.

Both men were also wearing com sets in their ears. He took one of those and put it in his ear. He didn't hear anything.

Sam went back to the closet, giving hand signals to Stella and quietly telling her to stay. She laid in the back of the closet as told and would herself wait.

Sam reloaded quickly and went to the open bedroom door. He listened for a while, but didn't hear anything. He lowered the optics for the night-vision and took a quick peek.

He didn't see anything on the stairwell, but his field of view was limited. He couldn't see much on the ground floor. The middle of the stairway would be a bad place to get caught if someone started shooting at him.

He went to the door leading to the upstairs balcony off the bedroom. It would be about a twenty-foot drop to the ground from there. It would be dangerous, even if someone wasn't waiting for him. He had a decision. He couldn't get stuck where he was. Stairs, or deck?

"I don't like this," Gillam said, pacing around the office. "There's no good reason Sam should be out there by himself. Here we are without any secure communications, we're blind, we don't know what's going on, and we don't have any protection."

"Don't worry about Sam," Debbie said. "He knows how to take care of himself. And if you want, I'll protect you."

Gillam looked at Debbie strangely, then began to laugh. It helped to ease some of the tension.

"Thanks, I'll keep that in mind. You've already saved my butt once."

"And I thank you, as well," Connie said. "It's a really nice one."

They all laughed, again.

"But really, I'm thinking I need to go out there and help in some way," Larry stated. "He might need me."

"For now, we need you," Connie said. "What if someone comes here?"

"I know. That's why I'm so conflicted. I can't be in both places at the same time."

Headlights were coming up the road to the main office. It was Bubba's wrecker.

"Until we know for sure it's Bubba, and he's alone, I want you girls to hide," Larry said.

A few minutes later, Bubba came in with several large shopping bags.

"Did everything go okay, Bubba?" Gillam asked.

"Yeah, I was able to get everything on the list."

"Did everything go okay, Bubba?" Gillam asked, again.

"Yeah, I told you..., oh, yeah, right. Banana split. Everything went banana split."

"Good. Girl's you can come out now."

When they came out, they questioned why he asked if everything was okay twice.

"I had given Bubba code words to use if things were okay or if things were not okay. Banana split was the good signal and hunky-dory was the bad one.

"Is Sam back yet?" Bubba asked.

"Not yet, and I'm worried," Larry said.

"Here are the phones you wanted me to get," Bubba said, handing Larry a bag.

Larry opened the bag, removing several sealed packages of pre-paid phones. "Great. They have to be charged before being used. Let's get them all plugged in. Did you bring food?"

"Of course, I did. That's what took me so long. The drive through was backed up."

"What did you get?" Debbie asked.

"Tacos. Lots of tacos," Bubba said, smiling.

"I beg everyone's forgiveness in advance," Gillam said.

CHAPTER 20

Sam had a plan. It might not be the best plan, but it would get him downstairs. Whether or not he would survive the night might depend on how well he executed the plan, he thought. Maybe he shouldn't use the word; executed, he thought again.

Sam had Stella guard the bedroom door while he prepared. He went into his closet and opened his bowling ball bag, removing the ball. He placed that by the bedroom door. He went to the bed and pushed off the large mattress, getting to the thick extra foam. Using a large knife, he cut a section he thought would work for his plan.

He heard whispering through the ear com, but it was in a language with which he was unfamiliar. He waited. He only heard two voices. He hoped that was all that was left.

He made sure all lights were out, then went and slowly opened the door to the outside. No one shot at him as he half expected. He put the cut foam over the door frame. Then went back and got his bag, placing both arms through the straps then over his shoulders like a backpack. He went to the bedroom door and pushed the bowling ball with his foot to the hallway. With the MP5 slung over his front, he grabbed Stella's collar. He pushed the ball hard with his foot, rolling it down the hallway where it reached and slowly started down the steps with a thud with each step. There was loud yelling on the ear com.

Sam, with Stella in tow, ran for the balcony door. As Sam reached it, he grabbed the foam and continued to where his motion took him over the railing, looking like a giant taco tumbling for the ground.

Stella was the lucky one, landing on most of the foam, but scared and whining as she headed for her doghouse. Sam was dazed, sore, but otherwise, uninjured. He was trying quickly to regain his senses and bearings, bringing the submachine gun up and ready to use. The ear com had popped out and the goggles had fallen off.

The bowling ball distraction must have worked, as there was no one outside shooting at him. He removed his bag and took cover behind his cut firewood stack, aiming at the open back door, waiting for someone to come after him.

Suddenly, bullets started cutting up the wood beside him. One of the assailants was shooting at him from the balcony he just took a flying leap from, but didn't have a good line of sight. He fired his entire magazine at Sam, and when he stopped to reload, Sam stepped out and fired. The man jerked, spun around, and fell backwards over the railing. He made a sickening sound when he hit the ground, but he never felt it.

Sam went to check him and started to reload when he felt the barrel of a weapon on his neck.

"Damn," he said. He knew he screwed up.

"Drop your weapon, hands on your head," a very thick accent, demanded.

Sam dropped the MP5. He knew it was coming. He put his hands on his head and closed his eyes, saying a silent and final goodbye to Debbie.

"No. Turn around. I want you to see this coming." Sam slowly turned. "Who are you?"

"I'm one who finally kills you. I win."

"I don't understand. Why me?" "Because you are—

A soft spitting sound followed quickly by what sounded like an egg having been dropped, sat on the air. The assailant's head jerked slightly and he fell immediately at Sam's feet. Sam dropped, grabbing the man's gun, scanning the area. From the inside of the back door, a lone figure emerged into the light.

"Hey, Lovett."

"Brenda?"

CHAPTER 21

"Don't forget to save some tacos for Sam," Debbie said. "He should be here any time now."

"There's a whole bag of them still," Larry said. "Bubba wasn't kidding when he said he brought a lot. But, then again, if I know Sam, maybe we should keep them away from him," Larry said, holding his nose.

"That's funny, that's exactly what he would say about you, Larry."

Everyone laughed.

"Larry, you said you were beginning to remember some things," Connie stated. "What do you remember?"

"It's a little cloudy still, things are coming in flashes. I close my eyes, try putting it together, like splicing in different parts of a jumbled-up movie." He closed his eyes and was silent for a few seconds.

He began again. "I can see, or sense I'm in a large room. I'm sitting. There's lots of bright lights. It's like I'm being interrogated. I'm restrained. Someone, a man, is asking me questions. A woman is injecting something into my arm. I don't think it's the first time. I don't see their faces. Someone did something to my leg where I got shot, but I don't remember if that was before or after. I can't move much, but I can turn my head. I can see the world. How did I get into space? I'm on a spaceship. I've been abducted by aliens. But it's just not right. There are no clouds and it's so clear. Now I know I'm not in space. I think what I saw was a large globe."

"You're in someone's office, I bet," Debbie exclaimed. "Do you recall what the man was asking you?"

"No," Larry said, opening his eyes. "I'm sorry. That's all I seem to remember right now. It makes my head hurt too much."

Connie put her arm around him. "It's okay, Larry. We'll get to it. Take it slow, bit by bit."

"You're wonderful," Larry said. "All of you."

"The main phone for the impound lot started ringing. At first, no one thought it would be a good idea to answer it, but Gillam told Bubba to go ahead. It was his business anyway and he was supposed to be there. It might even be Sam.

Bubba answered it. It was the night security guard at the main entrance. Doris was wanting to get in.

Bubba was about to tell him to tell her to go home. He would call her later.

Gillam interceded and told him to let her come in. They needed news about what was going on out there in the world. They might even send a message out with her.

Bubba told the guard to let her in, but make sure she was alone, check the trunk, and for her to park behind the office.

After a few minutes, Doris came to the back door and just

as she entered, she yelled for Bubba.

"Bubba, you better have those detectives in here and not another woman. Stop your hiding. Show yourself."

Bubba came out from his hiding spot. "Hey, Doris, this is a surprise. What are you doing here?"

"You know perfectly well what I'm doing here, but that won't happen now. You haven't answered my calls or texts and unless you have a good reason, I've got other places to be."

Gillam and the girls came out from hiding. "We're just being cautious," Gillam said. "You know what's been going on at the hospital and we're just trying to stay safe. Bubba is letting us stay here for a day or two. We had to take the batteries out of our phones just in case they were being tracked or listened in on."

"Where's Detective Lovett?" Doris asked, looking around.

"He went to get some firepower," Gillam said. "We're also a little defenseless right now, if someone knew we were here and came gunning after us, we'd be in big trouble."

"Tell me he didn't go to his house," Doris insisted, looking over at Debbie. "At least tell me he's not alone."

"I wish I could, Doris," Larry said, "I don't like it either, but he insisted. He thought it would be better for me to stay here since I'm a target."

"You don't understand," Doris began. "The attacks at the hospital were not meant for just you. They were after Lovett.

He's their main target, you're just a bonus."

"Wait, what?" Debbie exclaimed. "Why is Sam the target?"

"I don't have any answers about that," Doris said. "I only know the FBI interrogated the prisoner and got some information claiming that your husband was the primary target. I'm sorry."

"I need to go after him," Gillam said, moving towards the door.

"I'm going too," Debbie insisted. "Don't you even try to stop me,"

"I wouldn't. Bubba, don't leave, lock the doors, and turn off the lights. We'll take one of the burner phones with us and call you when we can."

"Wait," Doris said. "I need to show you something."

"We don't have time to waste, Doris. Can it wait?"

"No." she said. "Come with me." Doris went into the main office, the one that had been Granger's. She went to a large filing cabinet. "Help me move this," she asked of him.

Gillam pulled the heavy filing cabinet out from the wall. The cabinet had been hiding a cutout in the wall behind it. Doris reached in and pulled out two shotguns, handing them to Gillam.

"You are full of surprises," Gillam said.

"Doris?" Bubba said, stunned. "We're going to have to talk about this later."

Doris reached back into the hole and pulled out a small carry bag. It contained boxes of shotgun shells and a S&W.45

caliber semi-automatic pistol, fully loaded.

"This should make you feel a little better," Doris said, smiling.

Gillam handed one of the shotguns and a box of shells to Bubba. He walked over to Connie and kissed her. "Keep them safe, Bubba. We'll be back as soon as we can." He kept the .45 and gave the other shotgun and bag to Debbie. Together they went out of the office to find Sam.

CHAPTER 22

"Brenda, what the hell are you doing here?" Lovett asked.

"Apparently, saving your butt. Did Larry train you to leave your place of cover and concealment, and turn your back on an open door? I need to have a talk with that boy."

"No, he didn't, and ..., yeah, I know I screwed up."

"Well, at least you'll know next time. Oh, that's right, I made sure there will be a next time. You're welcome."

"Thanks, but why are you here?"

"I saw you leave the impound lot and knew where you'd be going. I also knew that these guys would be watching your house."

"You were watching the impound lot? Look, Brenda, I know you're not with the FBI. What are you doing?"

"Looks like you caught me. Okay, Sam, here's the deal. You're right, I'm not with the FBI. I'm with the DIA. I went to get Larry out of the hospital to keep him safe. I thought that when you found Larry gone, you would leave to go find him, but the assassination squad got there before I had a chance to get him out. You were still at the hospital. I couldn't warn you."

"I'm not following," Sam said, with a quizzical look. "It

wasn't just Larry they were after, you were the primary target. Everyone is after you."

"Now, that makes no sense at all. Why would they be after me? What's that got to do with Larry and why he went missing?"

"These guys were brought in just in the past several days. They were hired by a very powerful man. They knew you were at the hospital. They needed to get to you before tomorrow."

"Tomorrow? Why tomorrow? I don't have anything special going on. I've got Grand Jury in the morning, that's it."

"And who do you have Grand Jury on? Who are you trying to get indicted?"

"Just some low-life's who were selling drugs out of a clothing store downtown about a month ago. They had an operation set up in the back of their store. That's all."

"There's a little more to it than that. Two of the dealers are brothers of Omar Siran Muhammad."

"Never heard of him. Is he a dealer too?"

"No, he's one of the top private plastic surgeons in the country. His office is in a high-rise on Peachtree St. He has very sophisticated clientele. Many prefer to stay anonymous. He's innovative, rich, he can travel anywhere in the world without suspicion, and he is very well connected. We believe he has ties to several major terrorist groups. The brothers were stupid and had gone into the drug trade without their brother's permission. The store was one of the money laundering locations and a place to pass information for their organization."

"A plastic surgeon terrorist?" Sam questioned. "I've never heard of such a thing. Larry and a couple of others were taking the lieutenant's test that day. I led the raid with members from the squad. Why did they take Larry and not me?"

"There's much more we don't have information on. We believe they were trying to brainwash Larry into doing something, but he somehow escaped and then showed up at the Narcotics Squad."

"Brainwashed? Escaped? You know, you lied to us once about being FBI. How do I know you're telling me the truth now?" Sam demanded.

I would say you could ask him," she said, pointing down at the body. "Or, you could ask the one who was waiting for them in the car down the street, the one at the front door, or the one who is in the living room. Oh, that's right, they're all dead."

"Are there any more you haven't killed?" Sam asked.

"No, I think that's it, but watch your back."

"How did you get involved in all of this?" Sam asked.

"That's a long story. For now, it's classified. Maybe I'll tell you some day. But right now, let's get you back to the wrecker yard. I'm sure Larry's wondering what happened to you. Grab your toys."

"Stella," Lovett called out. "Come here, girl." Poor Stella came out of her dog house, looked around and went to Sam slowly.

"It's okay, girl. Are you hurt anywhere?" Sam started to rub her all over to make sure she didn't have any injuries.

Stella gave Brenda an ambiguous stare and a sniff, but otherwise seemed to know that she was not an enemy. Not sure if she was a friend yet or not.

They went back through the house, closing and locking the back door. Stella moved forward towards the living room giving that soft growl again. She came across the body of the one in the living room that Brenda had dispatched. She sniffed and backed away, turning and looking at Sam.

Sam went over and checked the body. His throat had been cut. "Good girl, Stella. He won't hurt anyone ever again." He turned to Brenda. "Did you have to make such a mess?"

"Well, excuse me. I didn't want to announce myself to everyone here. I mean I could have broken his neck, I suppose, but that wasn't a sure thing. I did what I had to do."

Car lights flashed through the front windows. Someone was in the driveway. It wasn't but just a few seconds later the front door opened, hitting against the other body lying in the foyer. Debbie was yelling Sam's name.

Stella couldn't contain herself and ran up to her as Sam came from around a corner.

"I'm here," he said. "What are you doing here?" She grabbed him and hugged him. Where's—

"I'm here too, you fool," Larry said coming through the door. "Are you all right? Looks like a battle zone."

Stella ran over to say hi to her human friend, or maybe trying to seek some kind words after all she had been through.

"We're both all right, thank you, very much," Brenda said, coming from the kitchen.

Larry brought up the .45 he had in his hand, pointing it at the emerging figure. Recognizing her, he lowered it, slowly.

"Are you trying to get yourself shot?" Larry asked, irritated.

"Well, not by you. That might be awkward to explain; shooting your ex-wife and all."

"I could claim self-defense," Gillam suggested.

"How about mental instability?" She countered.

"Okay, boys and girls," Debbie said, not letting go of Sam, "are we expecting any more house guests or a demolition crew?" Looking Sam in the eyes, she continued. "I want to know exactly what happened here, mister, but for now, I suggest we all get back to some place that's not likely to have a body in it."

"Brenda, do you have a car here, somewhere?" Larry asked.

"What? Do you think I beamed over, or I have a shuttle craft parked somewhere? Give me a break. Of course, I have a car. It's down the street."

Sam laughed. "No wonder you got divorced."

"Oh, we're not really divorced," Brenda said. "After Larry signed them, I never filed the papers."

Larry looked dumbfounded. "Wait, what? I thought—

"Gotcha," Brenda said.

"I think I'm starting to like her," Sam said. "Not to mention saving my life and all."

"We're going to have a long talk on the short drive back," Debbie said, her eyes narrowing at Sam.

"Debbie, you and Sam go ahead and take the car in the driveway, I'll get Brenda to take me to the car Sam drove over.

We'll meet back at the impound yard. Here, use these for now." Larry handed Sam one of the burner phones. "They're charged and already set up with each other's numbers in them.

Connie and Bubba have one too."

"What about me?" Brenda asked. "Am I chopped liver or what?"

"Here, stop your crying. I knew I'd run into you sooner or later. I got one for you too. That's before I learned you had lied to us, to me, about being with the FBI."

"Looks like we also need to have a long talk," Brenda said. "There is a lot to tell you. First and foremost, "I'm sorry.""

"Well, that's a start. But it's a felony to impersonate a federal agent. I'm not sure how to explain you."

"That's part of what we have to talk about," she said, looking over at Sam, and winking, "but, I'm sorry about everything. You deserve much more."

Larry gave a heavy sigh, "Okay guys, we need to get out of here. Sam, toss me your keys. Where's the car you were in?"

"It's on the back street, one block over."

"Call us if you have any problems or you think you're being tailed," Larry insisted.

"Yes, mother." Sam grabbed his bag, that now contained some new toys, curtesy of his now deceased home redecorators. "Come, Stella," Lovett called, as they headed out the door. "You stay safe as well. See you in a bit."

"Right. Do you want us to lock your door?" "Heck no. They'll just kick it in," Sam said. "Who will?" Larry asked.

"It doesn't matter. Bad guys, police, the neighbor's kid. I want to come back and have a door to close, and lock, so just leave it. You can close the one in the upstairs bedroom."

"There's going to have to be a report written somehow about this. We can't make these bodies just disappear."

"Yes, I know. I just don't want to deal with it right now. No more questions, no statements, hopefully, no more bullets. I just need to take care of Debbie, get us some rest."

"Okay. I'll call and get someone to remove the bodies at least. No need coming home to that smell."

"Thanks, Larry. You're a good partner." "Yes, I am. About time you realized it."

Shortly after Sam, Debbie, and Stella drove off, Larry and Brenda left the house walking down the street, headed for her car while keeping an eye out for any additional bad guys.

After walking for a few minutes, Brenda said, "My car is just ahead. I need to make a quick stop at this other one, if you don't mind. I've got to get something."

Brenda went around to the driver's side of a parked SUV. You couldn't see at first until you got closer, but there was a big man was sitting in the driver's seat. He looked like he had fallen asleep.

Brenda reached in the open window and removed a long, thin knife from the man's neck, wiping it off on his shirt.

"I don't think I really know you, do I?" Larry asked.

CHAPTER 23

Sam and Debbie arrived at the impound lot ahead of Larry and Connie. They went inside with Stella who got to experience a whole new set of people and smells, not to mention Cali.

Sam explained to everyone what had occurred at his house. There were a lot of startled expressions and many questions for which he had no answers.

Larry arrived first at the gate with Brenda right behind him. They turned their lights off. The security guard, having been advised by Sam, was expecting them, but using a flashlight, he still wanted to make sure it was them.

The security guard shone his light into Larry's face, confirming it was him, then went back to Brenda's car, checking it out just to make sure she was alone. He went back up to Larry's car and waved him through. Larry didn't move. The guard waved him through again, but the car remained still. The guard went up to the car and tapped it on the hood, waiving Larry through using his flashlight this time. There was no response. The guard went back up to the driver's window and looked in, Gillam was sitting there, his hands to his chest, looking straight ahead.

Brenda got out and went up to Larry's car. She tapped on the driver's window and Larry remained in the position.

"What's wrong with him?" the guard asked, concerned. "Is he having a stroke or a heart attack?"

"I don't think so," Brenda said. She tried to open the door. It was locked. She tapped on the window again. Nothing. She began to bang hard on the window. "Try the other doors," she told the guard. "Larry," she shouted.

"They're all locked," the guard stated.

Brenda pulled her gun and was about to break the window with it when Larry turned and looked at her. He shook his head a couple times and then rolled down the window.

"What's up," he asked casually.

"Are you okay, Larry?" Brenda asked.

"Ah, yeah. What did I do this time?"

"You spaced out," Brenda stated. "You were clutching your chest like you were having a heart attack. Are you sure you're okay?"

"Yes, I think I remember what happened to me. Part of it, anyway. Let's get up to the office. I'll tell everyone there what I remember, piece it together, and maybe we can all figure out what is going on."

"Is he going to be all right? The guard asked.

"Yes, thanks," Brenda said. "He just needs to get some rest."

"Is he okay to drive?"

"I'm sure. It's just a little way to the office. We'll be fine." She prayed they all would be.

The guard closed and locked the gate once they were through.

Gillam drove slowly to the office with Brenda following, keeping a close eye on Larry as they both parked behind it.

The sky was just turning the few clouds on the horizon a rustic red as they entered the office. It had already been a long day and night. There was much to talk about and plans to be made on how to survive another day.

William N. Gilmore

CHAPTER 24

Lieutenant Powell just got off the phone with Doctor Higdon. He was being sent to Detective Lovett's residence along with a CSI unit, a Homicide unit, and he had also contacted the FBI.

Detective Gillam called the lieutenant earlier on his way back to the impound lot about the incident at Lovett's house, to include the body in the car. He didn't give much information, but told him Lovett would make a statement later.

He also told him that they would be coming in and requested a security escort for Lovett to attend the Grand Jury hearing that morning. They would call back about the arrangements later, after they had some rest.

Rest, for any of them, was something hard to come by, but for now, they were safe, and that was something to be thankful for.

Sam and Debbie had that talk on the way back, and Sam was honest with her about what had happened, including how Brenda had intervened when he was sure he wasn't going to make it. She stopped and they both cried, held each other, and Debbie gave him a slap on the back of the head for screwing up, then hugged him again. There was a lot going on between them without much needing to be said.

Larry held Connie for a long time when he got back, but he needed to have a conversation with Brenda about many things. Then he would gather everyone, figure out some plans, and see where it went from there.

Brenda came up to Larry and Connie, "I know I have a lot of explaining to do, to both of you. If it's all right with you Connie, I'd like to talk with Larry first, then I'd like to sit down with you and tell you some things as well? You have nothing to worry about with me. Larry and I were a long time ago in a completely different world. He's yours and I'm happy for both of you."

"All right, but be honest. With both of us," Connie said, frankly. "He's going through a lot. We all are. Now is not the time for games."

"Fair enough," Brenda said.

"Let's get this over with," Larry said. "After you," waving his hand towards the unoccupied office.

Upon entering the office, Larry couldn't wait to get the first thing on his mind out in the open. "Why did you lie about being with the FBI? Why are you even here? And where—

"Do you mind if we go with one question at a time?" Brenda laughed. "I know you have a million of them, but I'm sure to forget some if you ask them all at once."

"This is serious, Brenda. It's nothing to laugh about."

"Yes, it is serious, Larry. And you have no idea what it all involves."

"Well, I'm listening."

"No, I'm not with the FBI. I'm with the DIA. I have been since we met. Well, almost. I was being recruited."

"Now, it's the DIA," Larry said, sarcastically. "I suppose you're deep undercover again and can't tell me anything?"

"I don't blame you for not believing me. It's a lot to take in. I was trying to protect my status and keep everyone safe, but I'll tell you everything. It's time you knew."

"This should be good. Go ahead," Larry said.

Doctor Higdon and Mutumbo were the first to arrive at Lovett's residence. The front door was unlocked and they went inside. What they found astonished them. What they found was nothing. No bodies, no blood, not even a bullet casing. The scene had apparently been cleaned by professionals. Very quickly.

They were now long gone, leaving just the faint smell of chemicals.

The CSI unit arrived and attempted to do their job, but if any evidence was to be found, it was already compromised.

Everything had been cleaned, possibly removed, and most areas were wiped down. There was no blood and there were no fingerprints found, not even of Lovett and his wife.

The SUV that was supposed to be up the street with the body inside, was gone. There were no indications anything had occurred there either. There were no witnesses coming forward.

Apparently, no one saw or heard anything. Unaware that anything had occurred until they saw all the various vehicles.

When the FBI arrived, they took notes and left. They didn't seem surprised. They had seen this before.

The only things which everyone wondered about, the things that didn't seem to belong, were the green and yellow polka dot bowling ball sitting in the middle of the living room floor and the mattress piece in the back yard.

CHAPTER 25

"Larry, I know there's a lot to explain," Brenda began. "I wasn't sure which way I wanted to go. I thought I would be able to handle both you and the DIA, but I was soon mistaken. I loved you, but this was my dream job, my future, and I believed it was my destiny."

"I thought I was your destiny," Larry said. "Why didn't you tell me? I was led to believe you were working in a lawyer's office. You would be working normal hours, coming home for us to be together. Why the deception?"

"It was just beginning. The lawyer's office was my cover and base. I didn't tell them about you either. But they found out and told me I had to make a choice. We were just starting out too, but we had only been together a couple of months. The proposal took me by surprise and I didn't think it through like I should have. I let my emotions rule. I think I wanted to hold onto a bit of reality in my make-believe world. But I couldn't let you in and I wasn't going to put you through that, so I left."

"You're going to tell me that you left, for me? You didn't think I could handle knowing the truth about who you were and what you did? You married me and left. How was I supposed to handle that?"

"I couldn't tell you. I couldn't make you a part of my other life. This is the real me, not the woman you fell in love with. I had to leave. There may have been consequences. Either for you or for me, maybe both. That's why you must never say anything more about this, about us."

"This is hurting my head," Larry said. "Let's talk about who and why they took me. I'm starting to remember some things. They still don't make a lot of sense, maybe you can shed some light on them."

"There was a lot of chatter going through the intelligence channels about Atlanta being ripe as a target for terrorist attacks, but there were also rumors about them wanting to experiment with a new tactic. We heard for years that kidnapping people of importance or authority and using them to get a device into a secure area might be tried. Of course, there was little chance of getting anyone to cooperate, so the thought was that they would use brainwashing or similar tactics on an individual. There are many who believe, because of your situation, that you may be one of those they intend to use."

"Brenda, you know me. I don't think I could be made to do anything like that. Me, brainwashed? I don't think so."

"See, that's something else our little, terrorist, plastic surgeon is known for. I think that's also how your leg got repaired. I'm not so sure you escaped as much as you were allowed to leave, after whatever it was they did to you."

"But none of that makes sense. I'm nobody and I don't

have any special clearance to get into anything that might be considered sensitive. And as for my leg, it looks good and feels even better. Did they put that in my head too?"

"I don't know," Brenda said, shaking her head. "Like I said, we don't have all the information we need. There are several agents working on it."

"Does it have anything to do with Lovett's Grand Jury and those guys he arrested who are part of that terror group?"

"We just don't know enough, yet. I'm sorry."

"I can't believe all this is over some guys getting busted for selling drugs out of a clothing shop. There must be a lot more to it. What have you got on it? You've checked their connections, families, all the usual stuff?

"Yes, of course," Brenda insisted. "It does seem overboard with what they are facing."

"Okay, let's go and fill everyone in on what we have and see if there are any ideas.

After everyone was caught up on what was known so far, and Sam giving details of the assault at his house, everyone was interested in what Larry was remembering.

"I'm seeing flashes of things," Larry said. "My car stopped on the country road and there was this light in the sky. It blinded me and then I had this awful stinging and burning in my chest, like I had been shot with a bolt of lightning. I recall voices, but not what was said. I was being raised into the air. I think I was lifted onto a helicopter."

"So, it weren't no UFO?" Bubba asked, disappointed.

"I wish it had been, Bubba, sorry. They were a different kind of alien. Once I was in the helicopter, I was injected with something. I don't how long I was out, but when I started to wake up, I found I was strapped to a table of some kind. It was swiveled so I was mostly perpendicular—

"You were what? What's a purple dic ..., what you said?" Bubba asked, giving Larry a funny look and blushing.

"Be quiet, Bubba," Debbie said, admonishing him, trying to stifle a snicker. "Let him tell his story."

"I was almost vertical, upright," Larry continued. "I couldn't see much. I had an extremely bright light in my eyes. I could see a little off to the side and I could see Earth, or what I thought was Earth. I think it was one of those fancy colored globes. I'm thinking I was in an office. I was starting to get a little clearer in the head when, I think it was a woman, tried injecting me again in the right arm. I tried to move and something happened to my arm. I think I screamed. She moved the table to have me lying flat. I don't know if I went unconscious or not. Things got real foggy. I'm not sure what, they did to my leg? I don't remember too much after that. Not yet, anyway."

"Do you think you would know the office again if you were there?" Brenda asked.

"I'm not sure. I only remember the globe. The woman is hazy at best. I'll try to remember more."

"I don't think trying to remember will bring anything back," she returned, "I think they will just continue to come out when they want, when something triggers a memory. But I have several ideas."

"I was afraid you were going to say that."

William N. Gilmore

CHAPTER 26

The Sun was just coming up as Doctor Higdon and Mutumbo returned empty handed to the ME's office. The private security guard who had been hired after the last fiasco was nowhere in sight.

"Maybe, he be in the back," Mutumbo suggested.

Doctor Higdon pulled the wagon around back to its usual parking location by the service entrance. Still no guard. The doctor opened the console and removed Betsy, his .44 caliber handgun, which he took with him all the time now.

"Why don't you wait here, Mutumbo, until I check it out and make sure it's okay."

"My place is with you, my friend doctor. We will check it out together."

After exiting the wagon, they made their way to the service entrance. The door was not just open, it had been forced open. Doctor Higdon did the smart thing and backed off. He got on his cell phone and called 911.

Within several minutes, police patrol cars and sheriff's units arrived, surrounding the building. Doctor Higdon and Mutumbo had taken a position behind the ME's wagon just in case someone came out of the building shooting.

"I have got to get that new security system installed and running," the doctor said. "We don't have anything reliable."

The building was checked and declared safe, before the doctor and Mutumbo were allowed to go in, even if the doctor was packing more firepower than most of the officers.

There were no living persons in the building, but the doctor was called to one of his examining rooms. On the table was a body covered by a sheet.

"I didn't leave it like this," the doctor stated. He checked the body under the sheet, and it was the security guard; dead.

Mutumbo came into the room after making his own check. "The shells of other bad men are gone, doctor," he declared. "All record files be gone too."

Doctor Higdon hurried into the lab only to discover that all the samples of the men were gone as well. Someone knew just what to take. The computers had also been wiped. He was furious. Not just with whomever may have done this, but with himself. He believed he should have been more careful.

This wasn't the first time the office had been compromised, but this time, it had been deadly. He called and talked with the sheriff, who reluctantly agreed to have a marked patrol car outside, twenty-four hours a day, and after talking with the County Commissioner's Office and the County CEO, there was the promise of a top of the line security system, with night vision capabilities, to be installed later that very day.

CHAPTER 27

"Anything?" Brenda asked.

The bright light was giving Gillam a headache and that was all. No flashes; no memories; nothing.

"It's not the right setting," Brenda suggested. "You're not under the same stress, in the same setting, and we don't know what drugs were used on you."

"But what about the episodes he had in his own office, the hospital, and when the guard outside put the flashlight in his face?" Connie asked.

"I just don't know," Brenda said. "He reacts to different stimuli, his surroundings, or both for unknown reasons. We can try to duplicate them, but only he knows what will work when it works. You can't force it."

"Then what are we to do?" Connie asked, throwing up her hands. "How can we help him?" Her voice breaking.

"I'm not done yet," Brenda insisted. "I have something else I want to try. It may be dangerous, even tip our hand, but it just might give us some answers. I think it's worth a try."

"If it gets me some answers, I'm all in," Larry said.

"With this, you may have already been in deeper than you ever wanted," Brenda said.

"What do you mean?" Larry asked, with a quizzical look.

"How would you feel about meeting with Doctor Omar Siran Muhammad, again, for the first time?"

Larry just smiled and nodded his head.

Homicide Detective John Starling met with Doctor Higdon at the ME's office. The situation was quite different from any other homicide he ever worked. The body was already at the ME's office, that also happened to be the location of the crime scene; if you could call it that.

Four bodies had been removed, a new one left, and items related to the first four, along with their case files, were missing, and the office's computers had files erased. All other evidence of anyone ever being there just didn't exist.

The 'scene' was cleaner than that of a hospital operating room. The victim, the one who was left, was the office's private security guard, laid out on one of the examining room tables meant for autopsies, and covered with a sterile sheet; one of the ME's own.

The private security company had been notified of the incident and a representative came to the ME's office and made an identification. The security guard was single, lived alone, and had no family in state. They would make any notifications if they could contact someone. If not, the company would handle the arrangements when the body was released.

Doctor Higdon was waiting for John to give the go ahead for the autopsy. There was nothing else to do.

As he hovered over the covered body, John asked, "Do you have an idea how he died, doctor?"

"Yes," Doctor Higdon replied. "Borrowing from my many years of experience in these matters, my professional opinion is that his heart stopped beating."

"Yes, doctor, I concur," John said, smiling. "I see the many years you devoted to your studies and all the money to buy the very best education in the medical field was not wasted."

"Well, that was in its simplest terms," Doctor Higdon laughed. "As to why it stopped beating, I'm getting ready to find that out if you will give me some space and a little time." He looked up at John, cocked his head and smiled.

"I'll just go now," John said, nodding his head. "I'll come back in a couple of hours."

"That's fine, detective," Doctor Higdon said, aware of the reasons why he didn't want to hang around. "You take your time, he's not going anywhere, at least, I don't think so; however, bodies do like to disappear around here."

Brenda called Doctor Muhammad's office. Using a fake name, she begged for an emergency appointment with him, saying only he could save her face after being bitten by a neighbor's dog. She upped the ante by saying she could pay any amount, in cash, and even threw in a couple names of his known clients as references.

After Brenda's begging, crying, then begging even more, the girl on the other end slipped up. Brenda was told he was out of the country, but should be returning within the week. If she could wait, he could see her next Tuesday. She should call back on that Monday to make sure he would be in and the time.

She thanked the receptionist many times, and she meant it. No one in the agency was aware that he was out of the country. The wheels and cogs in her brain started whirling. This might be the break they needed. Devious ideas came to mind.

CHAPTER 28

A ship was docking in the Port of Savannah; one that had traveled many miles on the open sea. It arrived right on time. The cargo; large, metal containers, full of cheap, manufactured goods, stacked so high, you would think the movement of the ship or a big wave would have them tumbling down into the water, sink the ship, or at least, cause it to capsize.

Somehow, these giant behemoths stayed afloat and delivered their goods without incident, day after day. This one though, carried something a little extra. Something that wasn't on the manifest.

He wasn't part of the crew and he wasn't a passenger. There were no papers, no passport, and no questions after the sizeable bribe to the captain. If the bribe hadn't persuaded him, or the demand was too high, he would make sure there would be a new captain to deal with.

He had been left alone, which was probably the smartest thing the crew could do, and he stayed to himself in his small cabin. Taking meals there, only coming out for sun and an occasional smoke. He filled his time with studying the information he had on his target.

Unlike the others, he would not fail. He had never failed.

This wasn't a mission or an assignment, this was a quest. The money was nice, but this was more than that. It was a sense of accomplishment, pride, and respect.

All his equipment was in one of those large, metal containers. Additional bribes had been paid to get it on and off the ship without documentation and inspection.

With the ship docked, the man made his way to his container. The process of removing the containers off the ship began. The very special container was lowered from the ship and placed on a waiting flat-bed tow truck. The truck driver had all the proper papers for the container, in the form of several hundred dollar bills, and without any problems, made it out of the dock checkpoint. He drove the truck to a preselected location that was secluded and out of sight.

The driver of the truck lowered the ramp of the truck, allowing the container to come off the truck slightly and driving forward, the container slowly slid off the truck until it was completely level on the asphalt.

The truck driver got out and went to the opening of the container and cut the secure seal that was meant to show the container had not been compromised. He opened the doors and there, just inside the container stood the man from the ship.

The man from the ship made sure the doors were opened fully, then re-entered the container. A few seconds later, a loud roar came from inside.

Pulling slowly out of the container was a bright blue,

early seventies, Chevy Impala. The man exited the car and walked back towards the truck.

The driver of the truck walked up and was admiring the old classic so closely, he didn't notice the man from the ship come up behind him until it was too late. The knife, long and sharp, sliced open so effortlessly the truck driver's throat.

He almost collapsed too close to the car, and the man from the ship grabbed him and jerked him back. He didn't want any blood getting on his Baby. That just wouldn't do.

"We can't stay here much longer," Gillam said, of the impound yard. "It's just not meant to be used as a safe house. Maybe we should come up with a plan to move to somewhere we can be safe and that has proper facilities."

"And where do you suggest we go?" Debbie asked. "I know, let's all go to my place. Oh, that's right," she said, sarcastically, while looking at Sam, "my place, my home, isn't a very safe place right now."

"Don't blame me," Sam said. "I was lucky to get out of there with my skin, thanks to Stella."

"Thanks to Stella?" Brenda busted out. "When did Stella learn to shoot?"

"What I meant," Sam stammered, "is that she alerted me bad guys were in the house. If she hadn't, I would have gone downstairs and met my fate there."

"Well, let's not argue about who saved who," Larry said. "Let's be thankful we're all together, safe and sound for now. We have a lot to think about and a lot to do."

"That includes getting me to the Grand Jury tomorrow," Sam said.

"You mean today, don't you, dear?" Debbie asked. "Is it tomorrow, already?" Sam asked, confused. "No, you doofus," Larry said. "It's today, already."

"Are you positive, Larry? It sure seems like yesterday."

"If either one of you asks, 'Who's on first?'," Brenda said, very seriously, "I'll shoot you myself."

CHAPTER 29

The drive to Atlanta from Sarvanana was uneventful. The packet on the seat next to him contained a Georgia license plate that was now on the back of his vehicle, maps, a driver's license, insurance papers, vehicle registration, as well as pictures and information on his quest. He had his own contacts to obtain such items and the resources to pay well for them. He didn't work for anyone. No one hired him. He was his own master.

The car was a classic for sure, but with a few added items which didn't come from the factory or that you would find in the local auto parts store. The trunk contained a secret compartment with various weapons, including a nice, break- down sniper rifle, several small semi-automatic machineguns, and some other rather nasty ordnance.

There were concealed items within the drivers reach which could turn him into a one-man army. The engine compartment as well as the driver and passenger doors had been enhanced with shielding to stop most handgun bullets, and it sat on self-sealing tires. There were many other features which made the car itself a fortress.

The man was well trained. Some might suggest he was former military; a mercenary, consultant, or contractor. He only did the jobs he wanted to do; not for profit, revenge, or any political or ideological reason, but now, for fun; for the adventure; for the rush.

He turned these into quests. Like knights of old, he believed they were noble, at least, in his own mind. Unlike the noble knights, innocents who got in the way, were dealt with harshly; witnesses were eliminated; the fair damsel was something to be conquered when there was time. The quest was always the priority. Nothing was more important than the quest; not prison, not even survival.

Larry and Sam met with Lieutenant Powell at an abandoned warehouse. They didn't want too much police action showing up around the impound lot. They wanted to keep it as a safe-haven for as long as they could; besides, the girls, and the non-human girls, were still there. Oh, and Bubba, too.

An armored SWAT truck would be used to take Sam to the Grand Jury with plenty of protection. As soon as they got to the courthouse, they would enter from a guarded underground parking garage and taken to the Grand Jury room where he would testify, then get him out of there and back into the truck.

Every step of the way, Lovett would be guarded. He would wear a bulletproof vest and a Kevlar helmet to and from the truck. SWAT units were on the roofs of the buildings around the courthouse.

Larry held back, not to be seen, but had insisted on being there. It's what partners do.

Lovett was getting warm in the back of the SWAT truck and took off his helmet to wipe away the sweat on his forehead. "Two minutes" the SWAT Commander yelled, from the passenger seat to the back.

Sam was sitting with a group of eight other people dressed just the same way he was. Black fatigues, helmet, gun belt, and semi-automatic rifle. He put the helmet back on. If you looked away and they changed seats, you'd never know which one was him.

"Thirty seconds," the SWAT Commander yelled, this time.

"You know what to do," one of the men in the back said. "Just follow our lead."

The truck came to a slight down ramp, a turn, and continued for a bit before it came to a stop. The rear door was opened and all the men exited. There was a line of four men flanked on both sides by two men. They were all hunched over, so size could not easily be made. They all quickly made their way to a guarded door.

Early surveillance, and maps of the surroundings allowed the man from the ship to set up and take advantage of the location. The shot might be difficult, but not impossible. He had made many, even more difficult shots.

He sighted through the high-power scope, adjusted for wind, and took careful aim. He took in a breath and let it out slowly, then holding it, checking his aim one last time, he squeezed the trigger.

CHAPTER 30

Brenda called one of her DIA contacts to check in, give an update, and to see if there was any intelligence chatter about Muhammad, his location, or his intentions. There was nothing. He was a ghost.

"But there is some disturbing news right now and we are working on it," the contact stated. "We're not sure if it involves anything which you are involved in or not."

"Okay. You're not going to make me try and guess, are you?" Brenda said, annoyed "What is it?"

"We believe an unauthorized individual was aboard a container ship that docked in Savannah yesterday. We also believe there was an unauthorized container onboard that somehow was allowed to be removed and placed on a flatbed truck. The truck transported the container to a secluded area, unloaded the container, and that is where the truck driver was killed. His throat was slashed. The container showed signs of having a possible vehicle inside.

"Do you have any idea who this joker is or where he came from?"

"We're checking and there has been no conformation, but the best guess is that this is the same person who killed a Saudi

Prince several years ago and the Japanese Ambassador in Australia last year. The M.O. is similar. A ship arrives and a large container is discovered. The body count starts to pile up. Sometimes the victim or victims are shot, sometimes the throat is sliced, and sometimes, a neck is broken. It's said he has his own agenda; he's not paid by anyone nor is he for hire. There is no money trail. He just shows up and soon, there's a body, or several."

"Is there not one photo of this guy? How about rumors, ideas, or even a good suggestion?" Brenda asked.

"We have nothing more," her contact advised. "What makes you believe he might be part of our situation?"

"Wherever this guy goes, there's death. With your report of foreign assassination squads running around, this guy may fit in that description too. He might only be one, but he's the one I would be worried about."

"Thanks," Brenda said, "we'll keep our eyes open."

"Careful," said her contact, "by the time you see it coming, it may be too late."

"One more thing," Brenda stated. "Is Area 51 still clear for use?"

"We can have it up and ready in about three hours, once I get clearance, but that may be the biggest problem. I'm not positive I can get that for you. You know how he is."

"Sure, you can," Brenda advised, "just tell him it's for me. He owes me."

"Should I call you with the details?"

"No, just leave the message on the usual location. I may have to ditch this phone."

"Roger that," the contact stated. "Good luck."

William N. Gilmore

CHAPTER 31

CLICK. The rifle's firing pin didn't strike a cap. There wasn't a bullet in the chamber. It was a dry-fire operation. There was no target, no victim, and no blood. This was a warm-up; an exercise to scout out and get comfortable with just one of the locations if he chose it.

He would do this with multiple locations. He would also track the weather for the entire week and longer if necessary; the traffic patterns, construction and work sites, escape routes, and any special events around the area of his operation, which might mean he would have to change the date, time, and location for his quest.

He was very thorough and he was in no hurry. He might even take time to go to a show at the Fox Theater, visit the Martin Luther King Center, or tour the Fernbank Science Center. He was also very cultured.

He broke the rifle down, placing each piece into the foam cutout matching the shape of the individual piece in the ordinary looking briefcase. Getting back to the street level and out into the bright light of the day and the smells of the city, no one paid any attention to him. After all, he was just another member of the crowd, blending in, nothing at all which would make him stand out.

Not only could he be a ghost when the need arose, he could become a chameleon, lost in plain sight.

The door leading to the courthouse was opened and all the men entered without incident. Lovett, safely inside, removed the helmet and the black SWAT jacket as well as the bulletproof vest. He still had the escort to the Grand Jury room.

He was immediately taken into the room where there were about twenty-three of the Fulton County citizens who had been selected to be jurors. The Assistant District Attorney gave a summation of the crime and then swore Lovett in.

Lovett gave testimony about the raid, the finding of the drugs, and the arrests of the men. It lasted only about seven minutes. There were no questions by the jury and he left the room. He waited for the bell to ring, which was to indicate there were no additional questions and the jury had voted.

The voting was not to give a verdict, but rather to say there was probable cause, or in other words, enough evidence for the case to continue in front of a Superior Court Judge. That's when the real court case begins. Negotiations between the District Attorney's Office and the defense attorneys; plea deals; time to serve; and other considerations. But that could be months down the road. The men were already out on a very high bond after their first appearance before a judge. Their whereabouts unknown.

If there was an effort to keep him from testifying, it would be a very nerve racking time, not just for him and Debbie, but for the team and the department.

Lovett had much on his mind, but for now, the only thing he wanted to do was to get back to his wife and his unborn child.

Gillam met with the SWAT truck at a different location after it was made sure no one had attempted to follow it. Lovett got in with Larry and together they drove off, eventually heading for the impound yard.

"How'd it go?" Gillam asked.

"You know Grand Jury, nothing special. I said my piece and got out of there. I don't think I even needed to be babysat. It went smooth."

"That's good. Do you really feel all this is just about them getting busted? I can't believe that's the motive, there has to be more."

"There's more all right. I just have to figure out what it is." "You mean, we, don't you partner. Somehow, I'm involved in all of this too."

"I think we all are. I've been meaning to talk with you about it too. Now that Debbie's pregnant, and what she has had to go through, I've been doing some thinking about what my next step is going to be. Where I want to go from here.

"You mean with the bad guys, right?" Gillam was getting a sickening feeling in his gut.

"Not just them, but with the squad, with the department."

"Woah there, pilgrim. Don't even talk that way. We have a good thing going. You can't leave. Where would you go? What would I do without you?"

"It's just something on my mind. I've got a whole lot more responsibility coming my way. I've got to keep my family safe. I want to see that little one grow up and he, or she, as well as Debbie, will need me coming home every night. That's job number one."

Larry couldn't argue too much about that. He never had kids. A couple of wives, but that was different. He drove silent, almost envious of Sam. He started to wonder where he and Connie were going with their relationship and just how far it would go. Time would tell.

CHAPTER 32

As soon as Larry and Sam returned, Brenda grabbed Larry and asked him to drive her to get some food for everyone. Connie was starting to get a little worried that Brenda was hogging too much of Larry's time. She trusted Larry, but she still wasn't too sure about Brenda. She would wait and see if it continued, and if so, would say something to Larry, or possibly take care of it herself.

Larry went over to Connie, put his arms around her and said. "Don't worry, we won't be gone long. Then we'll try to have some time just for us."

"That would be great if we could somehow have some privacy around here. Any idea how long we are going to have to stay here?"

"Not yet. We'll talk about it with everyone when we get back. I don't care where we have to go as long as I'm with you."

"I feel the same. Hurry back to me," she said.

Larry drove Brenda out of the impound yard and she gave him directions. They had passed many fast food locations already.

"Okay, Brenda, where are we really going?"

"We're going to get some food, but first, I need to go by

a location. Just trust me. I'll tell you all about it in a bit."

"Don't forget, trust is a two-way street. You've already taken me down a dead end once before. What am I supposed to believe?"

"I did save you and your partner's lives, didn't I? I mean, if you can't trust a girl after that, then what do I need to do?"

"Why don't you tell me what's really going on. Why is Sam a target? Why was I really taken?"

"I guess you deserve that," Brenda said, changing her tune. "They will skin my hide, but when we get back, I'll tell both you and Sam what I know. Turn here onto Piedmont."

Larry followed the directions, passing the Krispy Kreme Doughnut shop with the big, bright red sign; 'Hot Doughnuts Now'.

His mouth started to water. He might not drink coffee, but he could eat the heck out of those hot doughnuts. Not too far up, Brenda told him to pull over.

"Look down the street there and tell me what you see," Brenda said.

"Okay, I'll play along," Larry said. "I see the road, cars driving on the road, some buildings, a few billboards, some more buildings and some more road. Where are you going with this?"

"You see that one billboard, the one with the sleazy lawyer's face with the telephone receiver up to his ear?"

"He must be pretty bad not to have a cell phone. He'll run out of cord in a hurry chasing an ambulance."

"You see him winking?" Brenda asked, smiling. The billboard had electronic movement.

"Yeah, what of it?"

"Which eye is he winking?"

"The left one, wait, it's really his right eye. "Correct," Brenda said, patting Larry on the head." Do you see the number on the face of the phone base? Not the number to call him at the bottom."

"It's partially covered, but I see the numbers 3-3-6-2." "This is like one of our 'Dead Letter Drops'. We receive information this way sometimes. The billboard is a DIA plant. The attorney is real. It depends on which eye is winking and the number on the face plate as to what the information means.

"So, is this message for you, or what?" Larry asked, amused at the little ploy.

"It's for me. The guy's right eye is blinking, which is a go-ahead. So, we received the approval to use it."

"To use what?"

"We have a DIA safe house to move to once we get back. It's something I was able to arrange."

"Well, aren't you just filled with all kinds of surprises. I'm surprised you didn't make a call using your shoe. What's next, a flying car or an invisibility cloak?"

"Don't go overboard with any of this," Brenda pleaded, "I just want to help."

"If you really want to help, you'll tell us everything when

we get back to the impound yard. Don't hold anything back. No matter how bad you may think it is."

"I'll tell you and Sam," Brenda agreed. "The others don't have clearance."

"I can go along with that, for now. We need to head back. We still have to stop and get food."

"Okay, anywhere is fine," Brenda stated.

"I just need to make one quick stop." Larry said. "Trust me."

"Remember, a two-way street," Brenda said, cautiously. Larry smiled.

After picking up a box of hot doughnuts, Larry and Brenda stopped to get some real food for everyone. When they got back, they forgot to mention the doughnuts.

As soon as everyone had eaten, or rather, having to wait until Bubba was done, not just with his, but what he had offered to finish for anyone else who didn't eat all of theirs, Brenda gave them the news about the DIA safe house. It was north of Atlanta, a large house, secluded, fenced, guarded, and well stocked.

"It's called Area 51," Brenda stated.

"Of course, it is," Lovett said. "I'm not surprised. You could have used Moon Base Alpha, or Space Station Gamma and I would have known just where the idea came from. The UFO doesn't fall far from the mothership."

Debbie gave Sam a slight slap on the back of the head.

"What'd I say?" Sam protested, rubbing the back of his head.

"We'll take two cars. I'll lead. Stay together as close as possible. So that there's no problem, one animal to a vehicle." Bubba held up his hands counting fingers, then people, then animals. He looked at Brenda. "It's going to get tight in just two cars."

"There's no reason for you or Doris to go, Bubba. No one is after you. You are where you are supposed to be."

"How can you be sure?" He asked, almost pleading. "Detective Sam and Detective Larry are my friends. The bad guys might try to get them through me or know that I helped them and hurt me."

"That's not likely," Larry said. "No one has come here and you have twenty-four hour guards. I think you'll be okay."

"And besides, Bubba," Sam added. "The longer we stay here, the more likely they would find out and then come here. It's best you got rid of us now. You have a business to run."

"And we may need your eyes and ears out here," Brenda said. "You are our life-line to know what's going on. Without your help, we could find ourselves walking into even more danger or possibly a trap. You're big and strong. You make the chain strong. Just what we need so we can get back safe."

Bubba stood up straight, sticking his massive chest out, and smiling, saying, "I won't let the chain break. You can count on me."

"Good," Brenda said. She turned to all the others. "We leave in ten minutes."

———

CHAPTER 33

The man from the ship had many names. None which were close to his own. Every place he went, the documents; passport, license, all other forms of identification, had made up names which were never used again once he was finished.

He took on a persona that he believed would go with that name. It was like a game for him. If he believed the name sounded old, he would sometimes use make-up or prosthetics to make himself look old, walking hunched over, or with a cane. If the name sounded rich, he would take on an air about himself, sophisticated, with a well-to-do attitude.

Sometimes he would take names which were obscure in history, or turn famous names around, like the time in Amsterdam, he used the name, Gerald F. S. Fitz, a German car manufacturer. Which was taken and transformed from the author of The Great Gatsby, F. Scott Fitzgerald. In France, he once used the name Jules S. Sezar; a take-off on Julius Caesar.

He didn't strictly follow any certain religion or ideology, but was a student of many. Practicing or studying Buddhism, Judaism, Hinduism, and many others. He took care of his body and didn't drink alcohol except for the occasional dinner wine.

He had never married, didn't have a girlfriend, and made

sure his parents were well taken care of in their old age. He wasn't the one to party with, take bowling, or get into an argument with, but he was the one person who if you had a deep dark secret to tell, he would never disclose it, which is of course, until he needed to use it against you.

He was just leaving the Fox Theater having gone to a play. He had made the walk there from his hotel, stopping to enjoy a coffee along the way. He was now enjoying the evening and the delightful breeze as he made his walk back.

He had only walked a few blocks when he noticed a young man following him. He slowed his pace, observing the surroundings and the lighted and unlighted areas. He came to a crossroad, stopping for the traffic light, crossing to the other side of the road. The follower was only about ten seconds behind.

The follower had to wait on traffic, then crossed the road against the light. He had lost his mark. He didn't see him anywhere. He began to wave and two more young men ran across the street to meet him.

"Where'd he go?" One of them asked. "You were sending him right into the trap and now you let him get away."

"Yeah," the other said, "I bet he was loaded too. I told you we should have jumped him a block or two back."

"The outcome would have been the same," the man from the ship said, stepping out of some deep shadows. This way, you got just a few more minutes of breathing."

One of the kids pulled out a rather mean looking switch

blade knife, flicking it open. "Give us your wallet."

The man casually crossed his arms. "No."

"Give us your damn wallet and that fancy looking watch," he just spotted it on the man's wrist.

"No."

The look on the young man's face was something between surprise and astonishment. It was like he was wondering what he should do next. No one had ever said no to him and his knife.

"Don't play games," the follower said, "unless you want to get cut up real bad." He pulled his own knife out, a butterfly knife which he twirled around in his hand several times until the blade was pointed at the man.

"What's wrong," the man said, to the third young man, "won't they let you play with anything sharp?"

The third one, maybe all of fourteen, looking unsure, finally spoke up. "Shut up and give them your money, unless you want to get cut tonight."

"Ohhh," the man said, "Now you have me scared. I don't want to move. Come and get it."

None of the three assailants moved. All looking at each other, waiting for one of the others to step forward. Finally, the follower told the other one with the knife to get the wallet.

"Why me?"

"Just get it," the follower, demanded, obviously, the leader and possibly the oldest of the group.

The young man, maybe seventeen at the most, inched forward towards the man, giving him a wide berth, keeping his switch blade pointed at him.

"Boo," the man said, rather loudly, not moving and keeping his arms crossed.

The kid with the switch blade jumped back so fast, he dropped the knife. The others jumped too. The startled young man looked down at the knife then up at the man, then back at the knife.

"Well, aren't you going to pick it up?" The man asked.

The teenager bent down, but hesitated to reach out, half expecting the man to grab his arm, the knife, or both. The boy finally reached his knife and quickly grabbed it, backing up in a hurry, once again pointing the knife at the man.

"Let's get this over with, I have things to do," the man said.

"Throw us your wallet," the follower stated, "we'll let you keep the watch. Then you can go."

"No."

The follower weighed his options and couldn't look weak in front of his friends. He moved forward. Big mistake. He was quickly disarmed. The man spun him around to see his friends one last time as the butterfly knife, with about a seven-inch blade, spun blindingly quick in the man's fingers before it went easily into the area under the young man's chin, angled to the back of his skull. He dropped immediately.

The boy with the other knife charged in to help and had his knife quickly taken away, and stuck into his ear, up to the hilt, then twisted. He fell atop of his dead friend.

The third boy had witnessed the death of both his friends so quickly, he failed to run away. He was frozen in his fright.

The man reached down and removed both knives, wiping them off on the second boy's clothes. He put them in his pocket.

"Do you have anything you want to say?" The man asked the remaining unarmed, young man.

"He shook his head, not taking his eyes off his dead friends.

"Do you have anything to say to the police?"

The boy shook his head once more, then turned his face quickly to one side, bent over, and threw up. When he turned back around, wiping his mouth on his sleeve, the man was gone. He thanked God, and ran off.

The man continued the walk to his hotel. Shaking his head, he was talking to himself. He knew better. He shouldn't have done it. It wasn't like him at all. Why in the world did he allow that kid to live. Maybe he was getting soft in his old age. Maybe he reminded him of his brother.

William N. Gilmore

CHAPTER 34

The drive North went without a hitch. They all stayed together and only stopped once to get gas in both cars. It was always a good idea to have a full tank, just in case you had to bug out in a hurry, or needed a flammable liquid to make a Molotov Cocktail in the middle of nowhere. Containers, could always be found.

They drove down a dirt road to a large metal gate. There was no way to get around it. It appeared to open electronically. Brenda and Larry got out of their cars and approached a control box.

Brenda opened the control box. Inside was a keypad. "Go ahead, enter the code," Brenda said.

Larry looked at her as if she had two heads. "How the heck am I supposed to know..., wait a minute." He smiled, shook his head and looked back at the keypad, tilted his head a bit, then reached in and typed some numbers; 3362. After the last number was entered, the gate began to open. "The number from the billboard. The one on the old telephone face."

"Well, maybe you just might make a detective yet," Brenda said.

"Aren't you afraid your bosses will be upset with me

having the code?"

"It changes after every case. Just keep it to yourself for now. The gate will close on its own after the last car goes in, just make sure it does. And don't ever try to force it, it might just blow up in your face."

"You said there would be guards, where are they?"

"They are watching you right now, I believe. There are a number of hidden cameras. Men walking around with rifles would draw too much attention. Safe also means it should look as normal as possible, not like a Branch Dividian compound or a strange militia group."

They got back into their cars and drove through the gate. Just after getting through, Larry waited and saw the gate close on its own, just as Brenda said it would. They drove another half mile to a large, brick house. It had a circular drive in front and a drive that went to the rear.

Everyone was looking with wide eyes at the beautiful house. Most were expecting a shack, or even a trailer, hopefully a double-wide.

When they stopped and everyone was outside the cars, she went to the front door and knocked.

"Who's there?" Came a disembodied voice over the speaker beside the door.

"The big, bad wolf, and I'll huff and puff, and blow your house down," Brenda said.

"Not today, you won't," came the voice.

You could hear a heavy lock being disengaged, and then the door opened.

"Miss Brenda, how good to see you again."

"Mr. Williams," she said, stepping forward and giving him a big hug. "I'm sorry we have to intrude, but things have been a bit nasty lately."

"We received the notice, and, as is your usual way, Miss Brenda, with little advance, of course, but things have been prepared as best we can. Please, all of you, come in," Mr. Williams said.

Larry took a liking to him right away.

Once everyone was in the house, standing in the foyer, Brenda introduced the gentleman.

"This is Mr. Williams. He oversees your safety while you are here. You follow his directions if you want to stay alive. If you have concerns, tell him; if you have needs, tell him; if you have a problem with Mr. Williams, tuff. That is all you need to know at this point."

"Connie started to ask a question. "What if we—

"If you have anything in your vehicles that you may need, please get it now, put the vehicles in the garage in the rear, then return here. Thank you," Mr. Williams said.

"I suggest you do it," Brenda said, "and quickly."

Brenda handed the keys to her vehicle to Sam. Everyone scrambled back out to the cars to get the few items they brought, including the animals.

Larry and Sam drove the cars around to the garage, that had been opened for them, and pulled them inside. Sam was going to grab his bag of goodies from the trunk, but thought he would just wait a bit. He didn't want to tip his hand yet and he believed that it wouldn't hurt keeping a little secret.

"Who is this guy?" Larry said, laughing.

"Might have been in the army or marines, or as polite as he is, even a fancy butler for all we know," Sam chuckled, giving a salute, "Yes sir, pretty please, drill instructor."

"If you are done," Mr. Williams stated, "will you please rejoin us all in the foyer."

Sam, hiding his face a little, said "Sure, yeah, we're all done here."

"On the way," Larry added.

When everyone was together again, Mr. Williams passed a tray around. "Place all your electronic devices on the tray; cell phones, watches; credit cards with chips—

"You're kidding, right?" Connie said. "Credit cards?"

"They have electronic chips which may be traced," Mr. Williams said.

When everyone had placed the items on the tray, Mr. Williams added one other thing. "Now all your weapons, please."

"Now that's going too far," Gillam said. "We're here because—

"I know why you are here, Detective Gillam," Mr.

Williams said, "but this is now a DIA matter, we are in charge, and we will provide for your safety while you are here."

"Then I made a mistake," Gillam said. "It's time to go."

"And what of your friends, detective? Are you willing to put their lives at risk because of your hard head? Take them back out there where everyone of you is known, but you don't have any information about your very determined assailants? Not really a smart move, but if you insist, I won't stop you."

Gillam looked around; at Sam, Debbie, and Connie. It wouldn't be right to put them in that type of danger. Larry removed the .45 pistol and placed it on the tray. Sam removed his pistol and put it on the tray as well. Mr. Williams continued to look at Sam, holding the tray in front of him. Sam grimaced, bent down and took off the ankle holster and his. 38 caliber revolver, and put them on the tray.

"Dinner will be served in about an hour," Mr. Williams said. "You may find your rooms upstairs. There is a room for Detective Lovett and his wife, one for Agent Gillam, and one for Miss Connie. Detective Gillam, you have one of the bedrooms downstairs.

Larry began to explain, "Ah, Miss Connie and I—

"Are not married and it would be inappropriate to put you in the same room," Mr. Williams stated, looking the detective in the eye. "Not in this house."

"Yes, I mean, no, of course not," Larry said.

"The animals will be kept in the garage for the time being

where food, water, and bedding await them. Thank you." He turned and walked away.

Sam looked at Larry, "I think I may have been right on both counts, he's a drill butler."

Brenda took Larry off to the side telling Sam and the girls to go ahead upstairs and check out the rooms.

"Don't take it too personal," Brenda said, "he's one of our best and he's never lost anyone. He'll keep you all safe, or die trying."

I understand," Brenda, "but when it comes to protecting people I care about, including myself, I'm the one I trust the most. It's my responsibility."

"Then protect them by making the best of this. They're safe, you're safe. You don't have to worry while you're here." "But the bad guys are still out there. I can't do my job. All they have to do is wait. I need to find out who they are, get them before they have a chance to get Sam, or me, or any of us."

"We still have an appointment for Tuesday. We may find out more then. Just give us a little time. I promise, if we can't get a hold on this after that, we go in with both feet."

"Okay. We'll talk later once we get settled in. I'm not sure I like the idea about you playing the victim to get us into that office. I think I have a better plan."

CHAPTER 35

Doctor Higdon and Mutumbo had two young men in the examination room. Both had very little to say. Both were on autopsy tables, covered with sheets. Both had been the victims of someone who knew how to use a knife, or rather, knives.

The wounds to the young men were slightly different. One was from a long flat knife that had been twisted after entering the oratory canal and into the brain, while the other, from a slightly longer, yet thinner blade, had been pushed into the lower brainstem from beneath the chin.

Neither had defensive wounds, indicating the attack was quick, and, or unexpected. One boy, the one with the wound under the chin, did have some old cut marks on his right hand, but they looked incidental.

"I'm sorry to say that there were not any knives found at the crime scene," Detective John Starling said. "It looks like whoever did this, took the knives with them. I have some men checking the area to see if they were dumped somewhere."

"I do not think you find them," Mutumbo said, "I see wounds like this before with knives. They be professional; trained, someone not from here."

"Are you saying someone from overseas?" John asked.

"Yes. Training like this given to mercenaries and ..., to others. Silent, quick way to kill."

"I don't know if these boys were targeted," the doctor said, trying to get Mutumbo out of the conversation for the moment, "or if they just came upon the assailant, or saw something they shouldn't."

"Both these guys, even as young as they are, have long records," John said. "One of them has an assault with a knife. They even ran together. Could the knives have been theirs?"

"That's impossible to tell without them," Doctor Higdon said. "And even if you did find them, I'm not sure."

"Is there anything else you can tell me?" Starling asked. "The assailant, she, or most likely a he, is right handed and around six feet. Other than that, there was some bodily fluids found at the crime scene, someone threw up, but we are checking on that to see if it could have come from our victims or the assailant. There's nothing on the boys giving us anything else."

"Thanks again for your quick work, doctor." John said. "I'll be in touch."

John Starling headed back to the Homicide Squad. He couldn't get it out of his head; why would someone with professional skills take out two teenage boys? Were the knives theirs? Could it have been self-defense? In the ear and under the chin didn't sound like it, but then again, did the boy's try to assault their killer?

There were a lot of questions, but then again, there were a

lot of questions with every case. Too bad there wasn't a witness.

John planned to have their juvenile records pulled. There might be some information there. He would wait to talk with the families. He knew this was a bad time for them, no matter what the kids may have been into. He knew the pain and loss of losing a child. He wished no one else would ever have to go through something like that. He prayed that every day.

After Detective Starling left, Doctor Higdon went over to Mutumbo. "I know you went through a lot of things in your country before you came here, but sometimes, here, it's best not to give too much information about your past, especially if it's something that would cause others to think something bad about you."

I not be happy with things I do before," Mutumbo stated. "I have things in my heart I do not want God to see. I was taught things, done those things, and now, I want to do things good."

"You are good, Mutumbo. You will do great things for your people. You are no longer a soldier, you will be a healer, you will save your people, and you will be a great doctor."

"I have much to do to repent. I ask God to forgive me and to use me now."

For the first time, the doctor heard Mutumbo's big voice crack. He was afraid there was a lot more in Mutumbo's past that he didn't want to know and he was also afraid, not knowing.

The boy knew the man had come from the Fox Theater that awful night. He had to have a hotel within walking distance. That's where he was headed when they were targeting him. He just hoped he hadn't checked out yet.

He bet it was one of the big ones on Peachtree Street and set up early so he could watch the entrance to one as well as the area, just in case he was walking somewhere again.

He wore a big baseball cap and a hoodie, even though it was warm. He watched for hours; going into an ally to relieve himself when he had no other choice. He watched into the early hours, only leaving so he could get some sleep and something to eat so he could be refreshed to come back later.

He hadn't called the police, or told anyone about what had happened. The neighborhood was shocked, of course; the families devastated, swearing about how good the boys were and never in any trouble; questioning the police as to why they weren't patrolling the streets better and how they could let something like this occur.

He knew the truth, but he would keep it inside. He knew what had happened and somehow, had been spared. Was it because he had been unarmed, or was there some force which allowed him to live? He wanted to know, but did he dare?

CHAPTER 36

Mr. Williams cooked and served a wonderful dinner. Afterwards, everyone complimented him on it then were surprised with a delightful rice pudding for dessert.

When everything had been cleared, Gillam got everyone's attention. They all knew about the idea for Larry and Brenda to go to the office of the plastic surgeon. It would be just a reconnaissance, a fact-finding mission. No confrontations, no guns, no finger pointing, and there would be no back-up.

No one liked the idea and there was a loud jumbled discussion that turned into something a little bit louder. Mr. Williams came back into the large dining room and attempted to quiet the conversations. With no one listening or paying much attention to him, Mr. Williams left, but returned shortly. A loud pop caused everyone to jump, effectively stopping their talking in mid-sentence, and quickly turn towards Mr. Williams.

"Anyone for some Champaign?" Mr. Williams asked, with a smile. "Now that I have your attention," he said, going over to Connie first and pouring some of the bubbly into an empty fluted glass, "I believe there are plans to be made and cautions to discuss. You may get into the location you want, but it's always best to have a plan in advance as to how you are getting out."

"The man seems to know what he is talking about," Sam said. "Please, Mr. Williams, come join us. We could use a cooler head," Sam continued, looking at Larry.

Gilliam stared back, "Now don't you start—

"Gentlemen, ladies," Mr. Williams interrupted, "if we could discuss this with a civilized effort, we may even agree to some common idea. Otherwise, I have dishes to tend to."

"Don't let us interfere with your dishwashing, Mr. Williams," Larry said.

"I think you may want to listen to him," Brenda stated, "he is one of our best tacticians and he's been on more special ops than James Bond."

"Give the man a chance, Larry," Debbie said. "I'd like to hear from a real James Bond. It might save your life. And ours."

The talks kept civil the next hour or so, until there was something that could be called a plan. Without detailed blueprints or security information, they would be walking in almost blind. Unarmed, they would be vulnerable.

There were a number of contingency plans discussed, every one of them put their safety first. It was not an ideal situation, but both Larry and Brenda believed the information they may acquire outweighed the dangers they may face.

Only both of them walking out of the building, on their own two feet and alone, would tell.

John Starling was looking over the two boy's juvenile records and police reports on the crimes they had been charged with in the past when he received a call from Doctor Higdon.

"Hello detective, I have some news about the crime scene evidence which I thought you might want as soon as possible.

"Yes, of course, doctor. Thank you. What do you have?"

"The bodily fluid at the scene was bile, someone threw up, but it was neither of our victims at the scene. It wasn't there long. It could possibly be the suspects, but I doubt it. It contained pork and bread, beans and meat; a hotdog most likely from the mixtures of other items we found, but the other boys had similar items in their stomachs from a meal just before they died. I would say there were at least three boys out there, at least in my opinion. I hope that helps."

"It does. Another piece of the puzzle, Doctor Higdon.

Thanks for getting this to me."

"No problem. Let me know if I can help further."

"I will." Hanging up, John got back to the reports.

One of the boys had been charged with having a switch blade knife in his possession at school and later, had used a switch blade knife in an assault. Apparently, it was his weapon of choice, and possibly the type of knife that he had in his possession before it was stuck in his ear.

He seemed to hang with several boys who also liked knives. It just so happened that one was the other victim. He had a butterfly knife confiscated upon entering juvenile detention with the other victim when they were caught shoplifting.

People who owned butterfly knives liked to show off by twirling the knives around. Spinning them in their hand so as to have the blade go in and out of either side of a swivel handle, usually a metal one, then have two handles come together as one with the blade sticking out.

That's why the boy had old cuts on his hand; practice or showing off his skills with the knife.

"So, the knives were theirs," John said, out loud.

Further checking of the files indicated there was another boy sometimes associated with the two. Also arrested in the shoplifting and questioned at the assault, but not charged. John wondered if the boy liked hotdogs. He would soon find out.

CHAPTER 37

The morning was bright and beautiful; the air crisp and clean, with a slight fragrance of the wildflowers growing in abundance. An early mist hung over the landscape, slowly burning away. Mostly, everyone had slept and rested from the past week of excitement. It was like going on a bed and breakfast vacation. Except it wasn't.

Everyone was up, enjoying a big breakfast on the back patio, while Cali chased Stella in the tall grass. The group was going over last minute details. Very little could be added from the past couple nights of discussions.

Opinions during that time had varied from what to do or even if they should do anything. Both Larry and Sam, and sometimes Brenda, were very aggressive about going after whomever was behind all this mess, while Debbie and Connie wanted them to have some restraint, to wait, maybe even let someone else handle it.

After it was all said and done, Larry and Sam won out with Brenda being the tie breaker. Mr. Williams didn't vote, but would have gone on the side of being the aggressor rather than having to wait.

Afterwards, Mr. Williams took them to one of the first-floor offices. Inside were computers, printers, document machines, and a photography set-up. This is where passports, driver's licenses, and all types of identification, which could pass the closest scrutiny, could be manufactured quickly.

Identification was made for Larry and Brenda to match the names she had given to the doctor's assistant.

Larry and Sam kissed the girls, said their goodbye's, petted the animals, then went to meet Brenda in the garage. They got into Mr. William's car and left the safety of the house.

A little later, Mr. Williams drove Larry and Brenda to the city block of the high-rise building where the plastic surgeon's office was located. He didn't want to let them out in front in case there were cameras, which he was sure there would be.

Brenda, using one of the burner phones, had called the plastic surgeon's office again the day before as she had been instructed and an appointment was set up for ten o'clock, Tuesday morning.

She was also told to bring cash for the initial visit and would be told what the payment might be after that. Brenda had no intention of taking any cash, which she was sure if anyone had made any cash payment, it would have found its way into the hands of terrorists or some other nefarious group.

Brenda and Larry put the plan into effect and walked to the office building, going to the bank of elevators which took them to all the floors. There was one bank of express elevators which bypassed the first fifty floors and went directly to the next twenty floors after that. There was yet another one which took them to the top three floors. That's where they were going. A guard station for those floors checked you in, verifying your appointment, after that, you went through a metal detector.

Brenda, wearing a blue hajib to cover most of her dark hair, and top, and carrying a large open purse, showed their identifications which was for her and her make believe husband in their fictitious names. Her picture matched, but one of the guards took the identification picture meant for Larry and went up to him.

Larry, slightly hunched over and moaning, took down a stained scarf to show he had a large bandage over half his face, one that appeared to be oozing blood. The guard, surprised, quickly stepped back, grimacing.

"Please," Brenda said, "I have to get him up to see Doctor Mohammad. We are hoping to save his eye and his face."

"The guard, still shocked by the sight, almost throwing the identification back at Brenda, turned to the other guard, telling him to open the elevator.

Not wanting to turn to look at the poor, disfigured man, who was obviously in pain, he went to the elevator door that was just now opening, held the door open with his back to the pair until they had entered, wishing them luck. He gave a sigh of relief when the doors finally closed.

"Did you see that guy?' The guard asked the other, "Doctor Mohammad will have to work a miracle on him."

Larry and Brenda were moving quickly up in the elevator. There were bound to be cameras here and they didn't say anything fearing some kind of voice surveillance as well.

When the elevator stopped and the doors opened, they were met by a young lady who took them to a waiting room. There was no one else there.

"I was told we would be seeing Doctor Mohammad," Brenda stated. "We need to see him right away. My husband may lose his eye." Larry was holding his head down, still covered by the scarf.

"I thought you said it was your face that received the damage?"

"No. I said it was my husband. Maybe I did say it was me. I was distraught, frightened. I'm not sure what I said. What does it matter? We're here now. We need to see the doctor."

"He will be with you shortly. May I get you anything?"

"No, thank you. We just need the doctor."

After about fifteen minutes, the young lady appeared again. "Please, come this way, the doctor will see you now."

The young lady took them to a hallway which came to two large oak doors. She knocked, then opened one side, motioning them in, closing the door behind them.

Larry and Brenda found themselves in a large office, a beautiful, huge globe of the Earth was on the right side, a couch and deep cushioned chairs were in the middle, while a bank of windows on the left were open to show the city skyline.

There was a man at the far end of the room, sitting behind a desk. He stood, gestured with his hand towards the furniture.

"Please come in, Detective Gillam. It's good to see you again. Introduce me to your lovely ex-wife."

CHAPTER 38

The boy was watching the hotels in the Peachtree St. area again, hoping to get a glimpse of the man once more. He had been watching for several hours, changing his location from time to time, eating on an apple for breakfast.

If he didn't see him today, the man may have already checked out, he was wrong about where to look, or if the man was smart, had left right after the killing of his friends."

Even if he saw him, he wasn't sure what he was going to do. He wasn't going to confront him. The man was too fast, he knew how to handle himself.

It might not be a good idea to go to the police. After all, the three of them were trying to rob him. He didn't want his grandma to know and he didn't want to go back to juvy, or to adult jail.

"Who is this man?" the boy asked of himself. *"He showed no fear, no concern, no emotion at all, and he did it so easily. Why didn't he kill me?"* A tear fell down the boy's cheek. He was crying without realizing it, so wrapped up in who this man was, he forgot who he was for a moment. Not like him.

He promised himself right then and there, he wasn't going to be like that. Someone who could kill so quickly. Cold, unfeeling, uncaring. Then he realized he already had been. To his mother, his grandmother, his teachers, to life in general. He began to wonder how he could change.

Then he saw him.

Coming out of the hotel. Even at that distance, he was sure. Yes, that was him. Tall, dark, standing straight as he walked. Dark pants, a blue, long-sleeve shirt, his black shoes, polished to perfection.

The boy watched as the man walked down the street to a little coffee shop, went in, and sat down. He was able to see the man being waited on and soon brought a cup of coffee or tea.

The boy watched for a while and saw several people come and go until a heavy, balding man, wearing a rumpled, gray suit, his shoes scuffed and dirty, carrying a large manila envelope, went in and sat at the same table as the other man. The contrast was almost funny.

The second man, seemed to rudely brush off the waiter when he approached. Leaning closer to the first man, the second man appeared to say something, but did not seem to be happy in doing so, pushed the envelope to the first man, he received a smaller one in return, got up and hurried out of the shop.

The first man sat there, sipped his drink, and after about ten minutes, put some money on the table and left, walking back to the hotel with the large envelope.

The boy followed once more, but at a great distance.

Once, the man turned, looking around a bit, but there was

no way he would be able to see the young man, much less recognize him.

The man continued to the hotel, but did not go in the front entrance; instead, he went into the covered garage area. After a few minutes, only one car emerged. It was a beautiful, blue Chevrolet Impala. It turned onto Peachtree, passing the young man. With the driver's side window down, he was able to recognize the driver; the man; the killer.

Detective Starling arrived at the listed residence of Deshawn Richards. He went to the door and knocked. He waited for a bit and knocked again. He was just about to turn and leave when a he heard a series of locks being manipulated. When the door opened, a short, elderly lady, wearing a very bad wig and using a four footed walking cane, stood in front of him.

"Hello," John said, "I'm Detective John Starling with the Atlanta Police Department," showing his badge and identification. "Are you Ms. Richards?"

"What's the boy done this time?" She asked, her shoulders obviously slumping just a little.

"I'm not sure he's done anything, right now, I just need to ask him some questions."

"That's what they all say, just before they handcuff him and take him away."

"He may have seen something I'm investigating and he

could be a lot of help. Is he home, Ms....?"

"Mrs. Lumpkin. I'm the boy's grandmother, on his mother's side. He's not here right now. He may be along shortly if you would like to wait, but then again, he may not show at all. He has a mind of his own these days."

"Thank you," John said, entering the house. "It's pretty important that I talk with him."

"What was it he was supposed to see," Mrs. Lumpkin asked, as she showed the detective into the living room.

As John sat in an old cushioned armchair, he smelled the odors reminding him of his own grandmother's house. The smells which permeated throughout the house could only be associated with someone who habitually used tobacco and dip; which also infused into the cloth furniture and in the drapes over many, many years.

Carnival glass bowls and vases decorated cabinets and tables. Tapestries hung all around. She sat next to a very old Chihuahua laying on a stained pillow on the couch, the dogs tongue was sticking out at an angle, showing its severely, yellow-stained teeth, the few it had left. Ten years ago, the poor dog might have come yapping and snapping at his heals. Now, it was happy to breath.

"I'm investigating the death of two young boys over on Peachtree St. I think your grandson knew them.

"Oh, my, yes. Wasn't that a tragedy? I'm so glad he wasn't out with them that night."

"We're still not sure what happened or what led up to the incident. I was hopeful your grandson might have some knowledge or insight as to why the boys were on Peachtree St."

"Up to no good, I would say. I tried to keep him away from those boys. They were bad news, but he didn't have anyone else to look up to. He didn't know his father and he was an only child. The boy is smart and given a chance, he could make something of himself."

"I see his mother is in jail, when will she be out?"

"Never, I hope," the boy said, entering the living room. "Sorry, grandma," going over and giving her a hug. "We're doing just fine, the two of us."

"I'm Detective John Starling. Do you know why I'm here, Deshawn?"

"About my two friends who were killed. I heard you when I came in. I don't know why they were there."

"Well, I have a theory about that," John said. "Mrs. Lumpkin, would you mind if I borrow Deshawn for about an hour? I promise I will bring him right back."

Mrs. Lumpkin looked Starling in the eyes for a moment, she smiled, "I believe you, but it's not just up to me. I want Deshawn to be comfortable with this. I'll leave it up to him."

"Deshawn, I could really use your help."

Deshawn didn't want to look like he was being uncooperative in front of his grandmother. "You promise you'll bring me back when I say I want to, right?"

"Absolutely," John said, "I'll bring you right home. No arrest, no cuffs, no report. Just you and me."

Deshawn looked over at his grandmother. She nodded her head.

"Okay, but no longer than an hour," Deshawn said. "No tricks."

"No tricks," John said.

CHAPTER 39

"Did you do something to your face, detective?" The man asked.

Gillam removed the bandage and the facial prosthesis that made his face look damaged that Mr. Williams had applied earlier that morning. Brenda removed the hajib.

"Ah, I see. And how is your leg? By the way you are walking, I'd say the new experimental treatment I employed has worked."

"What else did you do to me?" Gillam demanded.

"I don't understand," the doctor responded.

"What did you do in my head? Why can't I remember anything?"

"The plastic surgery only took care of your leg. The problem in your head, as you say, involving you being shot by your own lieutenant, might best be handled by a psychiatrist."

"And there you go again," Gillam stated, "messing with my head. I know what you are doing."

"Allow me to let one of my staff explain further." Doctor Mohammad picked up his desk phone, waited a second then spoke into it, "Please join us if you don't mind."

"How is your partner, Detective Lovett, is it?" The doctor

asked while they were waiting.

"Still kicking and screaming. I think he would really enjoy meeting you. Or killing you."

A few seconds later, the door opened and a woman came in. Larry and Barbara turned, and as she walked towards them, Gillam recognized her, grabbed his right arm while taking several involuntary steps back. He almost fell over one of the big chairs.

"This is Doctor Greyson, a psychiatrist on our staff."

"Hello, Larry. It's good to see you again. How are you feeling? Are you adjusting all right?"

"You."

"Sometimes, the trauma of an injury or a disfigurement needs to be treated," she said, "as was in your case, but you left before your treatment was anywhere near finished."

"Luckily," Doctor Mohammad began, "I had finished with your leg, but wanted time to see the results. It's still a new procedure, one of my very own, I'm happy to say."

"Why don't you let us continue with the treatment?" Doctor Greyson asked.

"I remember things," Gillam said.

Doctor Greyson, her eyes widening just a bit, turned her head and looked at Doctor Mohammad. He gave an almost negligible shake of the head.

"There's no way I'm letting her touch me."

"Okay, we'll deal with that later. Why don't you let me

have a look at that leg? Has it healed properly?"

"You're not touching me either," Larry said.

"I think it's time we left", Brenda said.

"No, I think you should stay for a while," Doctor Mohammad said, then he spoke something in a foreign tongue, possibly Arabic.

As soon as he spoke, Gillam, stood straight, turned and faced the doctor. He apparently repeated the passage, but in English.

"The house of a tyrant is a ruin."

"That's correct Detective Gillam," Mohammad stated, smiling. "The house of your government is a ruin. Together, we will make sure America is a ruin."

Brenda wasn't going to have any of this, she grabbed Gillam's arm and said, "Let's go, Larry, I think we need to get out of here."

Gillam was like a statue. Brenda couldn't budge him and pulled on his arm several times. "Larry, what's wrong with you? We need to leave, now."

Larry didn't answer, in fact he didn't move an inch. "Detective Gillam, why don't you have a seat in the chair," Doctor Mohammad said.

Larry moved to the chair and sat down. He continued to look straight ahead.

"You've brainwashed him, haven't you?" Brenda asked, already knowing the answer." You son of a—

"His indoctrination wasn't complete before he left us. He has a very important mission to accomplish."

"The only mission we have is to get out of here," Brenda said.

"Good luck with that," Mrs. Greyson stated, laughing.

Brenda walked over to where Larry was sitting, standing between him and Mohammad, she looked him in the eyes. "Sorry about this, Larry", and then she slapped him hard in the face with one hand while the other, jabbed him with a pen containing a small needle in the other.

She hoped the mixture which Mr. Williams had concocted would bring Larry around quickly. She immediately pulled a small ball from her large purse, pressed a recessed thumb button, and tossed the ball to the floor.

White smoke started to bellow in the room while Brenda was already pulling Larry with all her might towards the doors.

"What's going on?" he managed to get out, while trying unsuccessfully to operate his legs properly. "I feel weird."

"He pulled his mumbo jumbo on you, turned you into Larry the Zombie for a few minutes."

They got to the elevator, but it wouldn't open. "Wait here," Brenda told Larry, propping him up against the wall.

"Like I could really go somewhere," Larry slurred, sarcastically.

The young lady who first met them when they came up, was sitting at a desk down the hallway. As Brenda approached her, she picked up a phone.

"Put it down," Brenda insisted.

She did.

"Give me your elevator key card," Brenda demanded. "The girl hesitated, looking down the hallway to Doctor Mohammad's office.

"You really don't want me to ask twice," Brenda stated, holding out her hand.

The girl opened a drawer to her desk slowly and reached in.

"If you pull out anything other than the elevator key card, I'll tear your arm off and beat you to death with it."

The girl's unsteady hand lifted out of the drawer and handed Brenda the key card.

"Now sit there, don't move, and don't you get on that phone for at least a half hour after we're gone. Clear?"

The girl slowly nodded her head.

Brenda got back to the elevator where Larry had slid down the wall and sat on the floor. She flashed the key card over the electronic control box and the elevator door opened. She was afraid it would be full of security officers. It was empty.

She struggled to prop Larry against the open, recessed door, so it wouldn't close. "Be right back"

"What, again?" Larry asked, a little more coherent.

Brenda knew what she was looking for and soon found it.

She pulled the fire alarm, and rushed back to the elevator.

The alarm would automatically send all the elevators to the ground floor A fire safety feature for tall buildings. She made it to the elevator, getting Larry inside, just as several guards appeared. The doors closed and the elevator rushed downward.

"Hurry, we don't have much time," Brenda said.

"For what?" Larry asked, shaking his head, trying to get clear.

"Plan 'E'. Get your jacket off." Brenda reached into her large bag and pulled out from a secret compartment, a blonde wig, quickly putting it on and stuffing her dark hair underneath.

Larry somehow got his jacket off which Brenda grabbed, turning it inside out to show a whole new color and pattern. She plucked a pair of glasses from the purse and put them on Larry. She also retrieved a large pair of sunglasses that she put on.

The elevator reached the ground floor and opened. The guards had other duties now. There was a large panic of people running around the lobby. The alarm was ringing while a mechanical voice was telling everyone to exit the building calmly and that the Fire Department was on the way.

Brenda, with Larry, who was walking pretty much on his own by this time, mixed in with the crowd and were making their way to the exit when a security guard grabbed Larry's arm. Larry turned and Brenda stopped, seeing the security guard who allowed them to go up on the express elevator.

"No, that's not them," the guard said, to his colleague, "The guy didn't have much of a face left and the girl was plain with dark hair. Keep looking."

Larry and Brenda made it outside into the bright sun and within a few seconds, a car pulled screeching up to the curb, barely missing some of the people trying to get away from what they thought was a burning building.

Brenda pushed Larry into the back seat and got in the front passenger side. Before she was fully in, the car driven by Mr. Williams, whisked safely away, leaving a blonde wig rolling in the street after them.

William N. Gilmore

CHAPTER 40

Detective Sterling and Deshawn were leaving the young man's grandmothers.

"Can I drive?" Deshawn asked.

"Funny" John said. "Get in the car. I promised your grandmother I'd have you back in an hour, and I plan to keep my word; times running."

"And no tricks," Deshawn added.

"That goes both ways, you know. I promised no arrest, no cuffs, so why don't you tell me the truth."

"Where are we going, anyway?" Deshawn asked, deflecting the question.

"You'll see. No tricks."

The quiet drive to the heart of the downtown area didn't take long.

"You hang in this area much?" John asked. "No, not too much. It's okay. Why?"

"I was wondering if there was a good place to eat around here. You hungry. It's on me."

"There's a good hotdog stand, not far from here. I sometimes eat there if I'm in the area," Deshawn said.

"And what would you be doing in the area, Deshawn?

Who would you be hanging with?" John asked.

"Just some friends," Deshawn said, "sometimes we come downtown to go to the library or to see some girls."

"Some girls," John said, laughing, "your what, fourteen? What would you do with a girl?"

"I'm almost fifteen and we get hooked up now and then." Deshawn pointed to a parking spot for John.

"I imagine your friends laugh at you. They're older, aren't they? More experienced?"

"I get around."

They exited the car and walked over to an open-air hotdog stand. You could smell the dogs cooking a long ways away.

"Let me see, I bet you're a mustard, relish, and chili kind of guy? John said, to Deshawn.

"That's right," Deshawn said, "How'd you know?"

"I'm a good detective."

"Yeah, right," Deshawn said, laughing.

John ordered for both of them, paying the vender. They sat along a concrete wall circling a young tree, providing shade.

"Tell me what you want to do with your life, Deshawn. What are your dreams?"

"I want to live it, be left alone, not bother anyone, and provide for my grandmother."

"What about school?"

"I go. I make the grades. It's a waste of time. Why do I

need to know about some guy that lived three hundred years ago? It's not the same world, it's not the same country, or even the same people. It all changes and it will keep changing."

"There are a lot of people out there right now who have changed the world," John said. "Maybe not famous or rich, but they work hard to provide for their families."

"They're suckers. I want to be famous and rich."

"Suckers? Like your grandmother?"

"No, not like her."

"Well, you call them suckers for working and providing. Isn't that what your grandmother has done. Isn't she now providing for you?"

"Only because my mother is in prison."

"And if she wasn't, you're saying your mother would take care of you?"

"I'm not saying anything. You're trying to confuse me. I could take care of myself."

"Yeah, I can see you taking care of yourself. In and out of Juvy, prison, drugs, robbing and stealing to support yourself. You have no idea what a Godsend your grandmother is. It's obvious she loves you very much and wants to make sure you are safe and you grow up right."

"Is this all you wanted to do? Come out here and talk?"

"No, I have one more stop to make, then as I promised, I'll take you home."

"Thank God," Deshawn said, "if this went on much

longer, I would have asked to borrow your gun so I could shoot myself in the head."

"Am I that bad?" John asked.

Deshawn just nodded his head as they walked back to the detective's car.

"Where are we going now?" Deshawn asked.

"Just up the road. When your friends were killed, do you remember them saying anything about where they were going or who they were with?"

Deshawn squirmed a little in his seat, readjusted his seat belt, and shook his head. "I don't know any of that."

John pulled over in an area on Peachtree St. and parked. He got out of the car. Deshawn just sat there. "Come on," John waved him to get out of the car.

Deshawn shook his head. "I'm good," he said, out the window.

John went over to the car and opened the passenger door. "I need you to see this. I have some questions you might be able to answer."

Deshawn slowly got out of the car, closing the door and leaning against it. "I thought you said no tricks."

"This isn't about a trick, it's about truth. You know what happened here, right?"

"This is where my friends died, isn't it?"

"I think you know that, Deshawn. I think you know exactly what happened here. Sometime after you and your two friends had gone to the hotdog stand, you came upon a man right here. Your two friends had knives; one was a butterfly knife and the other was a switchblade. They were taken away from them and used to kill them."

Deshawn's eyes were wide, his mouth open. He started looking around to see if there were any security cameras. How did this detective know so much about that night? About him?

"You saw this and you threw up your hotdog, right over there." John pointed to the area. "We know all this to be fact. No cameras, no witnesses, just pure science and detective work Why you were spared, or how you got away, we don't know. I don't care what you were doing here; I think this went beyond self-defense. The man was trained, experienced, but didn't have to kill. I care that there are two young boys in the morgue and the killer is loose. I think you care about your friends. Not what they did, or what they were doing, or even if it was their fault or not. I want to find the person who did this."

"What will you do if you find him?" Deshawn asked.

"I hope to find out why this happened, bring him to justice."

"What if they were trying to rob the man, wouldn't that be self-defense? Wouldn't he get away with it?"

"Not necessarily. But there are a lot of questions that need to be asked," John said. "There are two boys who had their lives cut short. They may have even been on the wrong side of the law at times, but they still deserved to live."

"I didn't have a knife," Deshawn said.

"What?" John asked, to see if he heard correctly.

"I didn't have a knife. I think that's why he spared me. I didn't run, I just stood there, when he killed them, I couldn't move, that is, until I threw up. When I looked back, he was gone."

"Can you tell me what he looked like?" John asked.

"I can do better than that."

CHAPTER 41

Larry and Brenda were back at the safe house, thanks to Mr. William's ingenuity. He had made a potion that had brought Larry back from La La Land and had orchestrated their getaway with a switch. Hide in plain sight.

"What was that you gave Brenda to inject me while I was under his spell?" Larry asked, rubbing his leg. "I don't even remember anything of what happened during that time."

"Then you don't remember me slapping you? Or jabbing you with the syringe pen?" Brenda asked.

"You slapped me? No wonder my face is sore too. We're going to talk about this later."

"Yes, I think we should," Connie advised.

"It's a secret, homemade formula to combat the brainwashing," Mr. Williams said, changing the conversation back. "It kind of jump starts your brain and snaps it back into place."

"You're a very talented person," Debbie said. "But we are still in the same old sinking boat. We've just changed cabins. When will all this be over? When can we go home?"

"I'm sorry, Miss Debbie, I do understand your position and your predicament. I hope to get you home as soon and as safely as possible That goes for all of you. Our agency is working hard on identifying the reasons behind the attacks as well as who is financing them, and if there is a way in which to curtail the activities."

"If? How about we just kill them all," Sam said. "I'm still not sure why I'm a target or who it is that's after me, so, let's just kill all the bad guys. The world would be a better place."

"What a marvelous idea," Mr. Williams stated and clapped. "Even if we knew who they all were and left a pile of bad guy bodies in our wake, their bad guy factory will just spit out more, even badder guys. Ones we won't know until it's too late. Let's play this out with our brains, not guns. Plan to win."

Sam just turned in a huff and walked away.

John got Deshawn back to his grandmother's house with very little time to spare.

"Here he is ma'am, on time and no cuffs," John said with a smile.

"I hope he was helpful to you, detective. He really is a good boy when he wants to be and he stays far away from those so-called friends."

"I'm hoping you don't mind, but I'd like to come back tomorrow and have Deshawn help me a little bit more. He's already said he would if it was okay with you."

"That would be grand with me too. I'd like to see a real

man in his life. Someone he can look up to."

"Well, this is a temporary thing. I don't mind checking up on him once in a while after my investigation is complete, but maybe we can get him enrolled into some activities that will keep him off the streets and give him a real goal and a positive outlook."

"Oh, I would be so proud of you, Keshawn," his grandmother said. "This is what I've prayed for."

"Okay grandma, I'll give it a try."

John said his goodbyes and left. Driving back to the office, he began to think. He was starting to see a pattern in his life now. He would be doing a lot more thinking in the days to come.

He called the Medical Examiner's Office, asking to speak with Doctor Higdon.

"Doctor Higdon, here."

"Doctor Higdon, this is Detective Starling, are you and Mutumbo going to be there for a while?"

"Yes John, I hope so, that is, unless we get a call for a pick-up, which I hope we don't. What's up?"

"Just need some help understanding how those boys ended up dead. I'll be right over."

John made quick time getting to the M E's office and met with both Doctor Higdon and Mutumbo.

"John, I'm not sure what more we can tell you. Both boys were killed with knives stuck into their brains. It was quick."

"Yes, it was, but did it have to be. Two boys, armed with knives, one at a time, they approached the killer. How did he disarm both boys so quick, there were no defensive wounds, no other cuts, or blood on the scene from the killer?"

"We are assuming," Doctor Higdon said, "that he may have had some training, either military or other."

"Mutumbo, you've had similar training, if I'm correct, when you were a soldier."

"I do not wish to speak of it" Mutumbo stated, flatly." There was no sign of those famous white teeth.

"I understand, Mutumbo, but what I want to know is if the boys were robbing or attacking the other man, could he have stopped without killing them?"

Mutumbo was silent.

"Mutumbo," the doctor said, putting his hand on the big man's arm. He couldn't reach his shoulder. "This is not in any way, a reflection on you. Your life is now, not what it used to be. You've made the decision to do good. Now let's do good by helping our friend out with what he needs to know."

Mutumbo took a deep breath, "The training, is not to stop, but to continue until there is no resistance, ever."

"Even if the victim is smaller and weaker than you?" John asked.

"Yes, it not matter."

"But could he have stopped. Did he have a choice?"

"Always choice."

Mutumbo went over to a desk and grabbed a pencil. He gave the pencil to Detective Starling. "This be knife. Try and stab Mutumbo."

John looked at the pencil with its sharpened graphite point, then at Mutumbo. Doctor Higdon was behind him. He turned the pencil around in his hand so that the eraser pointed at Mutumbo. He slowly approached Mutumbo, getting within just a few feet of him.

What happened next was a blur. John felt like he was on the Tilt-a-Whirl at Six Flags. He now faced Doctor Higdon and felt a big arm around his chest and the prick of a point under his chin. Mutumbo had him trapped with the sharp point of the pencil pushing uncomfortably against his skin.

"I have choice. Pencil in or pencil out?"

"Let's do pencil out," John suggested, quickly. "I get your point, no pun intended."

"That was something to watch," Doctor Higdon stated. "I've never seen a man so big move so fast."

"I have one more question. If there was a third boy there, unarmed, not trying to run away, what do you think the killer's reaction would be?"

"Not leave witness. Knife or no knife. But there be something you must know. This killer of boys, not here to kill boys. He is here to kill someone much bigger. I do not think it be with knife. And it be very soon."

CHAPTER 42

The next morning at breakfast, after everyone had a night's rest, the entire group went over what had occurred the previous day.

Sam still appeared to be a bit on edge and Connie wanted to know more about how Brenda came to slap Larry. She really wanted to know a lot more about their relationship, but wanted to be cautious of seeming to be too nosey, or jealous.

"We have to go back," Larry said. "We didn't learn enough about what's going on. Maybe we can get a search warrant and take a whole force with us, tear the place apart."

"We don't have any evidence to obtain a search warrant," Brenda stated, "they didn't do anything illegal while we were there that we can prove. If anything, I'm the one who threw a smoke bomb in their office and set off a false fire alarm."

"He hijacked my brain, isn't that enough?"

"Listen to yourself. Do you really want to tell a judge that? Not only will you not get a warrant, you might get a padded room. We have got to be reasonable."

"What was that you said he said in, what…, Arabic, that made me act like a zombie?"

"You repeated it right back in English. You said—

"Don't do that," Mr. Williams interrupted, "we don't know if it's a trigger that can be used in any language or only in one, or only by the person who first programmed him."

"Programmed?" Larry asked, "You think I've been programmed?"

"Most certainly," Mr. Williams confirmed. "That's what the DIA believed happened when you were taken. We have suspected Doctor Muhammad of being involved with brainwashings for a while. Some were possibly notable clients of his. In addition to the plastic surgery they received, they also were exposed to some kind of indoctrination, either to complete a certain task, or promote his cause. None of the clients would know and they all would have a trigger, or phrase that would activate them."

"So, what you are saying is all anyone might do, even by accident, is say this phrase and I turn into a robot, maybe a killing machine?" Larry asked.

"Well, not so bluntly, but yes, it's possible. According to what was said in his office, the indoctrination was not completed. We don't know what, if anything, you were tasked to do or when. It could already be in play or years down the line. I doubt it could happen by accident. It might have to do with not just the phrase, but who says it, even by phone. It could be voice activated."

"Is there any way to fight this?" Larry inquired, giving a look of hope, but knowing there was little to come.

"Without knowing a lot more, not right now," Mr. Williams said.

"If it's voice activated," Sam asked, "what happens if that voice dies before they can activate the trigger?"

"Then it should die with them," Mr. Williams stated. A phone rang and Mr. Williams went to answer it. "Agent Gillam, it's for you."

Larry started to get up, but Brenda held out her hand. "That's for 'Agent Gillam', if you don't mind," she said, smiling. She went in and took the call that was from her DIA contact.

After a lengthy conversation, she came back out and sat down. "I've got some more news as to why Sam was targeted. We confirmed an intelligence leak and it appears, the guys who you went to Grand Jury on; the guys selling drugs from the clothing store; the brothers of Muhammad; they put a hit out on you, but not just a hit, there is a sizable bounty to bring them your head."

"That still doesn't explain why I was brainwashed," Larry said. "How do the two interact?"

"That's still a mystery, but we're working on it." Brenda said.

In unison, Larry and Sam said, "Work faster."

CHAPTER 43

John picked up Deshawn at his grandmother's house early and took him to breakfast. The conversation was light until Deshawn asked John if he had any kids.

The many years of therapy and learning to deal with his own tragedy while surrounded by death almost every day on the job, helped when he told the story about his son, Peter. But it still touched a nerve and sometimes, while telling it, he would water up and his voice would crack, but it was important to get the story out. For some reason, he felt it especially important for Deshawn to hear. He even told him about Curtis and his aunt.

"You've been through a lot," Deshawn said, with a new impression of the detective.

"Yes, and so have you," John said. "I need to make a call to a friend of mine real quick. I have some more questions I think only he can answer for me about this man. Finish up your pancakes and we'll be on the way I'll be right back."

John went to the front entrance and called the Medical Examiner's office.

"Hey, Doctor Higdon, Detective Starling here, if you don't mind, I need to speak with Mutumbo again. I just have a question or two for him."

"I'm sorry, detective, he said he had some errands to do, so I gave him the day off. He'll be back tomorrow, unless it's that important and I can try to track him down. He doesn't have a cell phone."

"No. I was just hoping to clear up some things, maybe get a little more insight on the suspect."

"If he happens to come in later, which he does even on his days off, I'll give you a call."

"Thanks, doctor."

John went back inside and Deshawn was ready. He paid the tab and left a nice tip. Together they left for Peachtree St.

The man from the ship walked to the little coffee shop to have a cup. He sat at a small table having ordered his favorite and opened a newspaper. He slowly lowered the paper, seeing that he had been quietly joined by another person.

"It has been a long time, cousin," the man said. "I hear you are doing well and doing good work."

"I be well, work hard, and look ahead in returning to our country to do good there as well," Mutumbo said.

"I'm sure you will make our people proud."

"And will your killing of young boys make our people proud?" Mutumbo asked, looking straight into the other man's eyes.

"I was outnumbered, attacked, and unarmed," the man

stated bluntly.

"But you did not have to kill. They be just boys, small, untrained, with only knives," Mutumbo insisted.

"We were once boys; small, untrained, and we were turned into soldiers, taught not to hesitate, to kill those that would kill us."

"Why are you here, cousin?" Mutumbo demanded. "You need not worry, cousin, I am not here for you or any of our people. I have a quest. And then I will be leaving."

John and Deshawn parked in a parking lot where they could watch the hotel. Deshawn gave John all the information he knew about the man, including the car and the strange meeting he saw.

As they sat there watching, Deshawn had some questions. "Don't you ever want to stop seeing the killing, find something else to do?"

"Every day. I'm really close to retirement if I want, but being a cop, a detective, is all I ever wanted to do. I've been thinking about some things lately, started looking into them even. It's a big jump, but may be worthwhile. I've been thinking about—

"There he is," Deshawn blurted out, pointing through the window. "He's walking back to the hotel. He's with someone."

John saw the man Deshawn described. Actually, he saw

two of them, like a mirror image, only, he knew one of them. *What was Mutumbo doing with the suspect?*

John exited the car, telling Deshawn to stay in it. He drew his weapon and started walking the long distance towards the two men. Mutumbo was facing John while the other man had his back to him.

While they were talking in front of the hotel, Mutumbo recognized Detective Starling coming towards them. The recognition on Mutumbo's face caused the other man to turn.

He saw the man with a gun coming towards them, pushed Mutumbo, saying, "You did this?" and ran towards the parking garage of the hotel.

Detective Starling yelled out at the man that he was the police and to stop. He didn't; they never did. The man had a sizable lead on John and lost him in the garage.

While John was searching the ground floor of the garage, a car came down a ramp from an upper level, it's tires squealing on the pavement, going too fast for the curve. The car, a blue Chevy Impala, just as Deshawn had described, was now on the first level coming right at him. John fired several shots at the car and quickly got out of the way. As it passed, he fired more rounds at it, knowing he had hit the windows and tires, with no effect.

John was about to run back to his car when it pulled up at the garage entrance, Deshawn driving. John had left the keys in the car. When it stopped, remembering to put it in park, Deshawn jumped over to the passenger side.

John holstered his weapon, got into the car, and told Deshawn to get out.

"Go. You're going to lose him," Deshawn yelled, pointing in the direction the Chevy fled.

John put the car in drive and started to go, but thought again. "No, your safety is more important. I can't go after him with you in the car and I can't leave you here. It's okay, though, we'll get him."

"Who was that other guy who was with him?" Deshawn asked, looking all around and not seeing the man.

"It's someone I know. Someone I hope has good answers for a lot of serious questions."

John got on the phone and called dispatch to put a BOLO on the car with the information he had, to include the vehicle being bulletproof.

John had a uniform car take Deshawn home and told him he would check on him later. He called the Medical Examiner's Office.

"Doctor Higdon, has Mutumbo shown up yet?"

"Yes, detective, he just came in. He seems very upset over something, but he won't tell me anything. What's going on?"

"Just have him stay there, please. I have some things to do and then I'll be on my way to talk with you both. It shouldn't be more than an hour or two."

John went into the hotel and spoke with the manager. The room the man was registered in was identified, he was using an obvious false name; Juan Kenobe.

John had a SWAT unit respond as well as a CSI team. He didn't know what he would find.

The rooms adjacent to the suspects were evacuated. A pinhole camera was used to see if there might be anyone in the room. No activity was observed and entry was made. No one was found in the room.

The man apparently traveled alone, had just the basics in clothes and toiletries. He left very little behind which might be of use.in identifying him or what his intentions might be.

Fingerprints, samples which might contain DNA, and copies of video footage of the hotel areas covered by cameras were all collected, but nothing was of immediate use.

Then there was the car; where did he get that car?

CHAPTER 44

The man made sure he was not being followed, either from behind or in the air. He laughed at the face the policeman made as he went by, the bullets bouncing off his car.

The process was very expensive, the technology, revolutionary, but there was at least one more thing that the Nano-technology allowed. He made sure he was alone, before hitting the hidden switch just under the dash.

The car went through a metamorphosis and slowly changed color, front to back. It was no longer the beautiful blue, but now was a raging red. You had to love those Nanos.

Mutumbo must have gotten away. He couldn't believe that he would have set him up like that. He wouldn't. He tried to think it through and if not Mutumbo, who? Who else had knowledge he was in Atlanta? Not that funny little dweeb who delivered the documents. Not the..., of course, it had to be the boy. He had allowed him to live, now he became a problem. He had a way to deal with problems.

As soon as he completed his quest, there was the one mistake he had made which he would rectify. And he would never make the same mistake again.

And then there was Mutumbo. He knew what he was here

to do, he just didn't know the who he was here to do; or the why. It was best he didn't know. Mutumbo had changed. Those missionaries did a job on him. The same way they tried to do it to he and his brother, but they didn't have time for it. They were fighting for their lives; the soul could come later.

His brother; younger, more impressionable, willing to do anything for the cause, put himself out in front of danger too many times. Death was nothing more than a badge of glory.

During one firefight, a grenade was thrown into the room they were fighting from. His brother pushed him out of the way and kicked it across the floor, but not far enough. The blast caught his brother in the face, tearing open a ghastly wound, with tissue and bone exposed, destroying one eye.

Doctors were able to save his life, but his face was unrepairable. Several years of agony followed. The healing was slow, infections always there, headaches, dizziness, nothing anyone could do for him. That is, until a notable plastic surgeon took on the case.

After several months of treatment and therapy, he reappeared. His face had hardly any marks or indications it had ever been damaged, except for the one eye that always looked in the same direction.

The young man became a follower of this miracle doctor, almost always near him and his staff. One day, while he and his brother were at market, his brother received a call on his phone.

He listened for a minute, dropped the phone, said

something his brother didn't recognize, and walked off.

His brother tried to stop him, grabbing him, yelling at him, but it was as if his brother didn't know him, as if he were deaf.

They got separated in the crowd, the one brother calling out for the other, the one not hearing, or caring; he had to keep going, no one could stop him, nothing would deter him.

He kept searching the market for his brother, the crowds had gotten even bigger, but somehow, he was able to see his brother while looking down from another level. He yelled and yelled, but got no response. He started to go after him, trying to make his way to him through the throng of people.

Suddenly, everyone started running, knocking people down, spilling carts of goods. Someone yelled 'Bomb' and it got repeated over and over.

A lone, young man, his brother, was standing in the middle of the market with a suicide vest strapped to himself. Wires going to what appeared to be explosive charges circled his chest. He was holding a detonator.

The young man was yelling, but it was unheard due to the crowd yelling at him. Some yelled for him not to do it, some cursed, some cried, many were backing away.

Why hadn't he detonated it yet? He would have had the most impact a few minutes ago.

His brother made it through the crowd, stopped, begged for him to take his hand off the detonator. He said he couldn't, he wanted to, but he couldn't.

"Why are you doing this? This is not you."

"I have to do it. I'm going to do it. They have me. They have my face, my mind, my soul. I'm sorry, brother."

"Tell me, who has you? We can stop this." He began to step forward, towards his brother.

"Stop. It's too late." He held the detonator up. "Run." The crowd ran. All except his brother.

"You need to go. I will do this."

"No."

"Please, run."

"No."

"I love you, brother." He turned and ran himself, running to as safe and unoccupied area as he could before pressing the switch.

CHAPTER 45

Detective John Starling arrived at the Medical Examiner's Office. He went in and straight to Doctor Higdon's office where the doctor and Mutumbo were waiting.

"Now that you are both here, will someone please tell me what is going on?" Doctor Higdon asked.

John looked over at Mutumbo, "Maybe you better start. You know the story from the beginning and it may answer some questions for which I have lots of questions."

"When we be young, many members of our families become soldiers. We grow, we train, we fight together. Two of my cousins, they be brothers, become soldiers too. One hurt badly during battle and almost die. His face disfigured and lose eye. He suffer for many years. Then man say he can fix him, not make him see again, but face like before. He go away with man, long time, he come back face is fixed, except has eye that never moves. He become like disciple of man, follows him, until one day at market, he gets call on cell phone, disappears, and returns with bomb on his body. His brother tries to stop him, but he runs and blows up bomb, killing himself and others. His brother looks for people responsible."

"That's terrible," Doctor Higdon stated, "But what has

that got to do with what's going on now."

"Correct me if I'm wrong, Mutumbo," John offered, "but your cousin, the brother who survived, he is the suspect in the killing of the two boys?"

"That not be right," Mutumbo said, "he not be suspect, he told me he do it."

"What?" Doctor Higden exclaimed. "When did he tell you this?"

"Today when I see him. I go to find out why he is here, why he kill boys. The boys were to rob him. They had knives."

"I've got an independent witness to verify this," John said.

"You found a witness? Where? How?" Doctor Higdon inquired.

"The third boy at the scene. I'll tell you more later, after we find out what we can here."

"Okay," the doctor agreed. "Mutumbo, did your cousin say why he is here?" The doctor asked.

"No, he not say, but believe he know somewhere here in Atlanta, be person who made brother to blow himself up. If he find person, he not be stopped. He kill this person or die."

Gillam used the secure phone at the safe house to call Lieutenant Powell to give him an update and also to see how the investigation was going on his end.

"There's not any news on any other assault teams arriving here. You know the FBI, they're in charge and they are stingy with sharing any information, they haven't told us much at all."

"Okay, I'll call Starling and see if he can wiggle anything from his FBI contact."

Larry called Starling's cell, but there was no answer. He left a message to call him back.

He went and grabbed Sam for a talk. They went outside, away from everyone.

"So, what are your plans, what are you going to do when this is all over?" Larry asked.

"I'm still weighing my options," Sam explained. "Deb and I haven't talked a lot about it yet. I think I know what she wants, but I'm trying to wrap my head around it."

"She wants you to leave the department, doesn't she? But what do you want to do? You have a lot of time invested here. Do you want to throw that away? Is it fair to you?"

"That's the stuff we have to talk about. Maybe if I find something safer, spend less time on the streets, maybe even a desk job."

"And you think that will make you happy, stuck behind a desk?"

"If it makes her happy, that's what I want. Maybe later, when the kid is older, I can do something more."

"You'll be miserable, just to make her happy, and your

misery will spill over and you won't last five more years together, or there might be more kids. Then what?"

"We're stronger than that," Sam insisted. "We can handle anything as long as we're together."

"Yeah, just keep telling yourself that. It's easy to believe, until it's not."

"You don't know what you're talking about, Larry," Sam said, getting angrier. "You don't have any kids, you've only got that damn cat, so don't get high and mighty with me about what's best for my family."

"You think house training that idiot dog makes you qualified to raise a kid?" Larry said, way too loudly.

The door to the patio opened and out stepped Mr. Williams, Debbie, and Connie to see what was going on. Larry and Sam were separated by only a few inches.

"You know, I think you're just scared," Larry challenged. "I think you've lost your nerve."

Sam hesitated just a second "You're right, I am scared. I'm scared I won't be there to see my child grow up. I'm scared I'll leave a wife behind to have to raise our child by herself, I'm scared I won't measure up when the time comes, I'm scared that I'm not good enough." Sam started to tear up. "I'm scared that I will disappoint you."

Debbie started to cry. Connie put her arm around her. Larry swallowed hard and took a deep breath, "Never, partner. I was wrong. You have nerves stronger than steel. You're the best of both of us. There's no one else I'd rather have my back and there's no one I'd rather call my friend." Then Larry grabbed him and gave him a big bear hug. "I'm sorry I called Stella an idiot. She's pretty smart."

"Thanks," said Sam. "I think Cali is pretty special too. Maybe I'll let Stella teach her a few things."

Larry had his arm around Sam's neck as they joined the others on the patio.

Everyone went back inside. Sam was now comforting Debbie, and Connie took Larry's arm, holding him close.

"Detective Gillam," Mr. Williams called out, "headquarters says there is a Detective Starling trying to reach you with some important information."

"Can't he just call here?" Gillam asked.

"Wouldn't be much of a safe house then, would it? That's why headquarters handles all incoming calls. The secure phone here only handles outgoing calls."

Larry made the call to Starling, who was still at the Medical Examiner's Office. John relayed what had occurred with the two boys and how he got the information from Mutumbo about the person who killed them.

John told Larry about Mutumbo's cousin and how his cousin's brother had been brainwashed into committing a terrible act. How a phrase during a cell phone call had caused the boy to lose all self-control and become an instrument for destruction.

This was too similar to what Doctor Muhammad had

done to him. A phrase, when uttered by the doctor turning him into an obedient zombie, no will of his own.

Somehow, everything was connected. And it all led back to Doctor Muhammad.

"He's the target," Larry said. "Mutumbo's cousin is going after Doctor Muhammad. I'm not sure I really care what happens to him, but I still need answers. I don't see any way around it. We must go see him again."

After talking with Starling, Larry told everyone about the connection between he, Mutumbo, and Doctor Muhammad. He also insisted that they go and talk with him again.

"I'm not so sure that would be a good idea for you to go, detective," Mr. Williams said. "All he has to do is say the magic phrase and there's no telling what you may do. Possibly something terrible like what he had the other young man do. You could turn on your friends without even knowing it, or jump out a window of the high-rise."

"Well, we'll have to figure out something, because I'm going. No disguises, armed to the teeth, and this time, I won't be leaving until I get my answers."

"Then I suggest we prepare ourselves," Mr. Williams stated, "in the morning, but for tonight, we celebrate life. Good food, good drink, and good friends.

CHAPTER 46

John didn't know what to do with Mutumbo, if anything. He hadn't committed a crime and he couldn't make him stay at the Medical Examiner's Office. He hoped Doctor Higdon might talk with him.

He was going to head back to the office, but he had promised Deshawn that he would check on him. Before it got too late, he would drop in. Here was another situation he wasn't sure how he was going to handle.

There were three boys trying to rob the man, not two. Two boys were killed during the act. It really didn't matter if it was self-defense or not, a death occurred during a felony.

Deshawn could be charged not just with attempted robbery, but with the homicides of the boys. It was going to be a tough call.

He could talk with the District Attorney, try and get Deshawn a deal, but he wasn't sure he wanted to show his hand yet. Only a few trusted people knew there was a third boy, and he wasn't even armed.

"Why ruin a boy's whole life with this stupid mistake? He was worth saving, John knew it in his heart. He knew he had to try. There were so many boys who could be saved from ruin and heartache if someone would just give them some guidance, some hope, and some love, and once in a while, a kick in the pants.

John pulled up to the house, parking on the street. He walked up the lighted drive and to the door. Deshawn opened the door, inviting the detective in.

"I'm glad to see you're okay," Deshawn said, "that was pretty hairy there at the hotel. Were bullets really bouncing off that car?"

"Bullets bouncing off cars, you say," Deshawn's grandmother said. "Who was doin' the shootin'?"

"Yeah, grandma," Deshawn said. "It was a great movie, all these cop cars chasing this bad guy and bullets couldn't stop him."

"Youngsters," his grandmother said, to John. "All this 'Fast and Whatever'. Bad influence I say. Makes them want to go out and steal a car, go fast, and get themselves killed."

"Yes ma'am, I agree," John said. "If you don't mind, I'll take my leave, I just wanted to come by and see Deshawn for a minute. He's been so much help, I'm sure you're proud of him."

"More each day," she said. "And you come by anytime."

"I'll see you out," Deshawn said, "I'll be right back, grandma."

"I'll be waiting right here," she chuckled.

Deshawn and John went out on the driveway. "I almost blew that one," Deshawn said.

"Good recovery though," John said. "But I don't like to lie to your grandmother."

"Would you rather her think I was taken anywhere near a shooting?"

"Good point."

"Did they catch that guy?"

"Not yet, but we have a BOLO out on him and that car. That's a Be On the Look Out."

"Yes, I know," Deshawn laughed. "I watch cop shows. They are so fake though. Catch someone in an hour or half hour show. I had an uncle that was on the run for two years. Let's see them make a show about that."

"Here's my card. I wrote my private number on there if you need me for anything. Keep yourself straight, take care of your grandmother, and don't disappoint her, or me."

"Will you be coming back?" Deshawn asked, with a lot of hope.

"You better believe I will, and if I see you're not doing right, I'll..., well..., I'll kick you in the pants."

"Agreed," Deshawn said, smiling.

They shook hands without saying anything further and then John went back to his car.

Neither one saw the classic Chevy, sitting just around the corner. It had followed John at a distance from the Medical Examiner's Office to the location of the one he had allowed to get away.

John had an in-home dinner date with Dorothy while Curtis was spending the night with some of his friends. It was the first time they would really be alone and have the house to themselves.

John stopped to get a nice bottle of wine, but wasn't sure which type to get, one for dinner, or one for after. He was about decided on both when his phone rang.

"Hello."

John could hear someone on the other end, but couldn't make out what they were saying.

"Curtis? Is that you?"

In a very whispered voice John strained to here, the caller said, "It's Deshawn. He's here, the killers here."

CHAPTER 47

Doctor Higdon and Mutumbo sat in his office just after John left. Not much was being said, until the doctor made a rather interesting comment.

"Why don't you take the day off tomorrow, Jacob. I have a student who needs some extra credit coming in. It seems you have a lot on your mind and have some things you might want to get done."

Mutumbo looked at Doctor Higdon, hesitating for just a second before answering. "Yes. There be much weight on my heart. I be sad I not stop my cousin for killing boys, but I not be sad he find person who kill his brother. I not be sad he will kill them. Am I wrong?"

"I'm not sure there is a right or a wrong to that," Doctor Higdon said, shaking his head. "I can understand wanting to take revenge on them for what they did to his brother, but then again, he kills young boys without hesitation, without thoughts of their lives, of their families, of his own soul."

"He not be worried about soul. He not be worried about others. He only be worried about not finish what he be here to do.

"And that's to kill the person who caused his brother to

blow himself up," Doctor Higdon said. "That's that plastic surgeon, Doctor Muhammad?"

"Yes."

"Are you goin to try and stop him?"

"No."

"So, what are you going to do, Jacob?"

"Stop him from killing other boy."

"The other boy? You mean the one Detective Starling talked about? The third boy at the scene? The witness?"

"Yes"

"Why would he want to kill the boy if he let him live when he killed the other two?"

"He make mistake."

Doctor Higdon got on the phone and called Detective Starling. Starling answered, giving him information that he believed Mutumbo's cousin was already at Deshawn's house. He gave him the address and hung up.

Doctor Higdon unlocked a drawer in his desk and pulled out 'Betsy', his .44 Blackhawk. "Come on, Jacob, your cousin may be trying to kill the boy now."

They both ran out to the Medical Examiner's van, Doctor Higdon trailing a little behind, a little out of breath, but ready to jump in and head out. Mutumbo was already in and with his seatbelt fastened. The doctor tossed 'Betsy' into Jacob's lap.

"Will you use it?"

There was no answer. Mutumbo was looking down at the

holstered weapon in his hands. He hadn't held a weapon in a very long time; promising not to after becoming a Christian.

"Jacob," Doctor Higdon called out, taking a curve just a little too fast, but maintaining control, "are you willing to use it against your cousin?"

"No."

"Not even to save a boy's life?"

"I not use gun, not on anyone. I make promise to God."

"Okay, Jacob, it's okay," the doctor stated with understanding. "Just hold it for me while I drive."

Deshawn was downstairs with all the lights off. His grandmother was upstairs asleep. He knew the man was outside somewhere, he saw the shadows, heard the bushes rake against the house although there was no wind.

He was hiding downstairs in the kitchen, this time, he had a knife; one of his grandmother's big butcher knives. He didn't dare move or risk calling out to warn her. He would have to stop the man from getting to her.

He was scared. He didn't want to die. He wondered if this was how his friends felt before..., before they died. It was quick for them, barely having time to take a breath. Maybe it was better that way, he thought. He hated being scared, having to wait to see how he was going to die.

He heard more noises just outside the kitchen. He braved

a look out the window and saw him. He ducked down so fast, he almost stabbed himself with the knife.

John arrived at Deshawn's house, barely coming to a stop before jumping out. He ran straight to the front door, gun drawn. He tried the door, it was locked. Banging on the door, he yelled out, "Deshawn, it's John, open the door. Deshawn, open the door." He was about to bust it open when it finally opened.

Deshawn stood there holding a big knife. He dropped it and jumped the short distance, putting his arms around John's waist.

"Where is he? John asked, looking inside, gun ready. "He was outside by the kitchen. I saw him."

"Okay, we'll check it out. You stay right here."

"No. I want to stay with you," Deshawn trembled, still holding onto him.

Doctor Higdon and Mutumbo came around to the front of the house.

"That's him," shouted Deshawn, burying his face into John's chest.

"No. That's just Jacob Mutumbo and Doctor Higdon. Friends of mine. You saw Jacob at the hotel. Remember?" Deshawn, pulled away from John. "That's not who I saw. I saw the other man."

Suddenly, a noise inside the house got everyone's attention. Deshawn's grandmother was coming down on the stair-lifter, her ugly dog was in her lap, and she was holding a big, double-barreled shotgun.

"When I said, you could come back anytime, I didn't mean for you to show up with a bunch of your friends in the middle of the night, Detective John Starling," the elderly lady said, with scorn, "but if you're going to have a party, don't you think you should invite the homeowner?"

"We're sorry we woke you, ma'am," Doctor Higdon offered, "We thought Deshawn was in trouble—

"He might be in a bit of trouble now, just like the rest of you. Making all that racket. I need my sleep and so does Precious, here," she said, patting the mutt on the head.

"We'll only be a few more minutes, Mrs. Lumpkin," John said. "We just want to make sure, everything is all right, inside and out."

"Whatever you think is best. You're the detective," she said, putting the lifter in motion, going back upstairs.

"Okay, it's obvious no one got into the house," John stated, but we'll check the area around the outside of the house, again. I'll get a flashlight."

Doctor Higdon already had a flashlight and was checking the grounds. He came across something he wanted the others to see. All the others, except Deshawn.

"Hey, Deshawn, can you go back into the kitchen and look out the same window and show us where you saw the man," Doctor Higdon asked.

Deshawn looked up at John. John nodded his head.

"Okay," he said, a little unsure, but headed that way.

While Deshawn was on the way inside, Doctor Higdon showed the others several fresh and very large shoeprints left in the soft dirt by one of the other windows.

Deshawn tapped on the inside of the kitchen window and was pointing to a spot very near where they were.

"I not be in that area, before now," Mutumbo said. "Those not be mine."

"Someone, big and heavy, was here very recently," Starling said. "I'm afraid we may know who. I don't know his intentions, but I have a guess. I think I'm going to stay around here tonight."

"We can stay too, if you wish, detective," Doctor Higdon said. "Strength in numbers and all." He patted 'Betsy', now strapped to his side.

"Thanks, but I'm sure we'll be fine."

CHAPTER 48

Deshawn told his grandmother that Detective Starling was going to stay the night. She insisted that Deshawn tell him that she kept her bedroom door locked and her shotgun cocked.

John made sure all the doors and windows were locked. He also put a stack of aluminum pots against each door to the outside as an early warning system.

He made sure to call and explain to Dorothy why he had to blow off dinner and how bad he felt. She said she understood and wanted him to be safe. She would look forward to other dinners alone in the future.

Deshawn gave John a pillow and blanket before going off to his room. He returned a few minutes later.

"I'm sorry I was there," Deshawn said, his voice a little shaky.

John knew exactly what he was talking about; being there on Peachtree St. with the other boys.

"Then I guess it won't ever happen again, right?" John asked.

"I swear, I won't," Deshawn promised. "I don't want to ever do anything bad again. I want my grandma to be proud of me. I..., I want you to be proud of me."

"Deshawn, for what you have had to deal with, the realization and acceptance of the wrong you were doing, and what you have done for us so far, I am very proud of you."

Deshawn ran and gave him a hug, for the second time that night. Afterwards, Deshawn went back to his room and John, sitting on a smelly, old couch, started thinking about his future again while keeping an eye on the door. His hand resting on his weapon under the blanket.

Doctor Higdon and Mutumbo reluctantly left John at Deshawn's house, knowing that the man who killed two boys was now apparently trying to make it three.

He had been at Deshawn's house, that was obvious, but what had scared him off? Had he and Jacob arrive just in time, or did he see Detective Starling? Maybe grandma with the vicious dog on her lap, shotgun at the ready, riding to the rescue, got to him. Doctor Higdon gave a chuckle under his breath thinking about that one.

Just as they were crossing an intersection on a green light, the wagon was hit, spinning it around several times, almost tipping it over. There had been no screeching of tires as someone tried to stop in time, no blast of a horn, just the roar of a powerful engine, and the sickening crash of two vehicles colliding.

The air bags deployed, but the side impact caused Doctor

Higdon's head to strike the driver's side window, busting it out and rendering him unconscious.

Mutumbo's airbag kept him from receiving more severe injuries, but it broke his nose. Blood was all over his face. He unfastened his seatbelt and leaned over to check on the doctor. He was breathing, but unresponsive. He got out of the wagon and went around to the driver's side.

A car slowly drove up and stopped, headlights just now turning on, shining on Mutumbo. Jacob put his hand up to block the bright lights and to see who it was. He had a pretty good idea already.

His cousin stepped out of the car; the re-enforced body and frame barely suffering any damage. Walking up to Mutumbo, He took his scuffed chin in his hand, turning it side to side.

"I think your nose is broken, cousin" he said, "but I think it gives you character.

"Why you try to kill us? Mutumbo asked. "I must get help for Doctor Higdon, he be hurt bad."

"I'm not trying to kill you, you know that. If I wanted you dead, you both would be dead.

"Why hurt Doctor Higdon, he not do bad to you?"

"I'm just sending a message. To all of you. Leave me alone. Let me do what I came here to do."

"I know you want revenge, but I ask you go, not do this."

"You know it's right, besides, it will solve a lot of

problems for all of us. It's going to happen one way or another."

"And the boy?"

"That's just unfinished business. I had a moment of weakness. My reputation is on the line, I'm correcting it."

"It be finished when you let him live. Now it be my business. You forget boy, I forget you."

"Interesting, but what about your friends?" "I speak for me, they speak for them."

"I'll consider it. Now, get your friend some help, and tell your other friends not to get in my way. Next time, anyone of them may not be so lucky. And don't worry, I won't hang around, I'll leave once it's done."

He headed back to the car and Mutumbo turned and reached into the broken driver's side window. He grabbed 'Besty' from the holster on the doctor's right side, turned, and took aim at his cousin just as he was getting into the car. He couldn't pull the trigger, and the car roared off. He got Doctor Higdon's cell phone and called 9-1-1.

CHAPTER 49

Larry snuck up to Connie's room in the middle of the night, careful not to make any noise on the stairs. He lightly tapped on her door. He heard some noise and turned the knob slowly. The door was unlocked and opened slightly. The room was softly lit from an almost full moon shining through the window.

He called in softly. "Connie, are you awake?" He heard muffled sounds coming from her bed and saw some movement under the covers in the muted light.

"Connie, darling, I'm here."

The covers on the bed were thrown off, revealing Connie and Mr. Williams in a naked embrace. They began pointing and laughing at him.

Larry was wearing one of the explosive vests. He held the detonator in his right hand, his thumb touching the button. He heard a phrase in his head, repeated over and over again, being spoken by Omar Muhammad. He had no choice. He had no will of his own. He pushed the button.

Larry jerked awake. He was in his own room, downstairs, alone. His heart was still racing from the dream, the nightmare.

He felt around his body. He was still wearing the vest.

He looked around once more and saw that his bed was surrounded by little, grey aliens with big eyes. They were all talking to him telepathically, all talking at once, together in his head like a swarm of bees, until one slightly taller grey got right into his face and yelled, "Do it.". Again, he pushed the button.

Larry awoke, thumb twitching. Quickly feeling and looking around his body for the explosives, relieved this time, they were not there. He hoped he was awake.

He took a cold shower, shaved, and went down to the kitchen. Mr. Williams and Brenda were there discussing something. They stopped when he entered.

"Good morning, Detective Gillam," Mr. Williams greeted him. "I hope you slept well."

He tried not to let the dream, still fresh on his mind, bother him, nor let it show. "My brain was pretty active last night. So much going on, I guess."

"That happens sometimes," Mr. Williams responded. "As I recall, you are not a coffee drinker, would you like some tea this morning?" He held up a steaming tea pot.

"Do you have any milk?" Gillam asked, having a seat at the table. "I think I'd just like a nice cold glass of milk."

"Of course," Mr. Williams got up, going to the refrigerator "You and Miss Cali have the same breakfast appetites today. She and Miss Stella have been served and are outside right now."

"Thank you for taking such good care of them. I know

Sam and Debbie appreciate it too."

Mr. Williams placed a large glass of milk in front of Larry who downed almost half of it in one gulp.

"So, are you two making secret plans for today? Will we be repelling from a helicopter and through a window or parachuting onto the roof?" Larry asked, being snarky.

"We could," Brenda said, "either one. Which would you prefer?"

"How about we just stay out of the air. I've had my fill of helicopters," Larry said.

"When were you in a helicopter?" Brenda asked, fishing for some information.

"When they first picked me up," Larry said, as a matter-of-fact without realizing it. "It was quiet. It was as if it didn't—

Brenda and Mr. Williams were listening intently to Larry's story. "Go on," they both said.

Larry shook his head. "That's all I seem to remember at the moment. I don't know where that came from. It just popped up.

Brenda was smiling. "That's it. That's how he does it."

"Who? Does what?" Gillam asked, confused.

"Muhammad. He's got a stealth helicopter stashed somewhere. That's how he gets out of the area without us noticing. Either it's a big one or it takes him to where we won't be monitoring and hops a plane when he travels overseas. No passport to be stamped, no customs, and no inspections."

"He could get just about anybody or anything in or out of the country," Larry said. "From drugs, cash, terrorist, even a nuclear bomb."

"I'll call headquarters for help," Mr. Williams said. "We need to find where that helicopter is being housed."

"It most likely wouldn't be in a heavy populated area," Brenda said, "someone would have noticed it, maybe even complained about it. It may be in a large building or hanger on a large piece of rural private property. It could even be in a barn."

"I think you touched on it, Brenda," Larry said. "Being a stealth helicopter, is there an area that is getting calls about UFO's, strange aircraft, vibrations, even black helicopters. Calls from some nut jobs who are being dismissed. Most county sheriffs know who the kooks are in their areas who keep calling about weird stuff and those that rarely call, but now are seeing things. Get them to start checking the county sheriffs and police in a bullseye circle going outward from Atlanta. I don't think it would be further than fifty miles away so it could be accessed quickly if need be.

"Great idea, Detective Gillam," Mr. Williams said. He hurried to the secure phone.

CHAPTER 50

John awoke to the smell of bacon frying. He was laying on the old couch with the blanket over him. On top of the blanket was Precious, her tongue hanging out and those big eyes staring at him.

He lifted the blanket up and slid out, leaving the dog on top and set it back on the couch. He put his shoes on and holstered his weapon before going into the kitchen.

Mrs. Lumpkin was cooking while Deshawn sat at the kitchen table, finishing his breakfast.

"Good morning," John said.

"Good morning," Deshawn returned.

"And good afternoon to you, Mr. Rip Van Winkle," Mrs. Lumpkin stated. "Do you always sleep this late?"

"John quickly looked at his watch, horrified that he may have slept so long. It was nearly 7:30. He looked at Deshawn who gave him a wink.

"Sit yourself down, Detective John Starling. How do you like your eggs?"

"Over easy, thank you."

Deshawn was shaking his head, giving a smile.

"Three eggs scrambled coming right up," Mrs. Lumpkin

announced. "How do you like your bacon?"

"Ah, crisp?" He said as a question more than a statement while looking at Deshawn.

Deshawn nodded his head. The smile was bigger. "Milk or orange juice?

John looked at the glass by Deshawn's plate. "Milk it is."

"Milk is for a growing boy. I think you might be the orange juice type," she said.

Deshawn couldn't hold it in anymore and began laughing.

John had to laugh too.

"Two silly boys," Mrs. Lumpkin said, shaking her own head, "sitting in my kitchen, laughing their fool heads off. What am I going to do?"

That just made Deshawn and John laugh more. Then John saw the shotgun standing in a corner of the kitchen and the reality of why he was there set in once more.

The Emergency Room doctor came out of the treatment room and met with Mutumbo.

"He's still unconscious and may have a concussion," Doctor Menzell said "The x-rays show there's no abnormal swelling or fracture, so that's good news. The primary factor is his age, but he is fit and there are no other health problems."

"He be better soon?" Mutumbo asked.

"I believe he will be. I've known Doctor Higdon for a number of years and I know that he will fight. He won't want to miss too much of all of this, so he'll come around soon, I'm sure. He'll have to stay here for a while, though. We'll do some tests when he wakes up and make sure he is okay."

"I don't believe it be time for Doctor Higdon to go to his reward yet. He has much to do. I have much to learn."

"We will take the very best care of him we can. He's one of us. You both are."

Mutumbo went outside, still in possession of Doctor Higdon's cell phone, he tried the number listed for Detective Gillam, but there was no answer.

He then tried the number for Detective Starling. After a few rings, it was answered.

Mutumbo explained to John what occurred after they left him. Several times, John needed to get him to repeat, but understood most of the information; enough for him to know that he should start for the hospital.

He hated to leave Deshawn and his grandmother alone, but believed he was in good hands. He said goodbye and went to his car.

The car was lightly covered in the yellow pollen that covers everything in the Southern spring and summer months. He got in and was about to start the car when he saw something disturbing.

On the dark hood of the car were several very distinct,

large handprints in the yellow dust. Almost like a fingerprint powder, it caused them to stand out much bolder.

John got out of the car and got down, looking under the car where the handprints were located. What he saw chilled him to the bone. There were several wires leading from the engine compartment to a package duct taped to the underside of his car, right under the driver's seat.

John stood back up, shaking, backing away from the car.

He put the keys into his pocket, deep into his pocket. He went back to the house and had Deshawn and his grandmother, along with little Precious, leave out the back door and go to a neighbor's house. When he was able to compose himself a little, he called for the Bomb Squad.

CHAPTER 51

It was going to take a while, maybe a long while, to start getting information back from the counties that were being searched for the stealth helicopter.

In the meanwhile, Mr. Williams was preparing for the next confrontation with the plastic surgeon. Besides the cocktail which he made for Gillam to help counteract the effects of the brainwashing, he had a few other tricks in mind. He was being assisted by Sam and Debbie, keeping them busy, their minds occupied, while Larry and Connie were going over maps. All the rural roads and trails made Larry think of something.

Hey, Mr. Williams, a helicopter is going to use a special type of fuel, right? I believe it's referred to as avgas. So, what about deliveries to out of the way places by companies that supply avgas?"

"I'll pass that along," Mr. Williams stated. "Maybe they can cross reference the information and get a better pinpoint."

Brenda walked into the room, the expression on her face said she had some bad news.

"Doctor Higdon and Jacob Mutumbo were injured in an apparent attack. Mutumbo is all right, but the doctor has not regained consciousness yet and is at the hospital."

"Oh, my God," Sam said, "what happened?"

"Mutumbo's cousin rammed the Medical Examiner's wagon. He got out and told Mutumbo for us to back off."

"Like that's going to happen now? I don't think so," Gillam said.

"There's more," Brenda said. "Detective Starling's car was found to have a bomb attached to it. He was parked at the home of the boy who was the witness from the incident on Peachtree St., also involving Mutumbo's cousin.

"He gets around," Debbie said, "but isn't he also going after that plastic surgeon doctor? Why not let him? Let him take care of that problem for us. Keep our hands clean."

"I understand where you're coming from, Debbie," Larry said, "but allowing someone to commit a murder is not 'keeping our hands clean'. Not only is it wrong, we don't get the answers we need and we're not sure that will stop any of us from being targets."

"I thought he was a terrorist," Connie said, "that wouldn't be murder, would it?"

"I might have to agree with Connie on this one," Brenda said, "I think it might be a national security matter, in the best interest of the nation and all."

"Mr. Williams, you seem to be the voice of reason here," Connie said, "what do you think about all of this?"

"Well, he's still a US citizen, there has been no warrant issued," he looked over at Brenda who rolled her eyes, "there's been no indictment, and no solid proof presented that he is a terrorist."

"Other than brainwashing my partner for some evil reason. Okay, so we know where you—"

"I'd say, let him kill the bastard," Mr. Williams exclaimed.

Several mouths opened in surprise and Connie said, "Oh, my."

Sam laughed.

"Then which one would be the real terrorist?" Debbie asked.

"If we allowed that to happen," Larry said, "we would be the terrorist."

The all clear was given and Starling's car was now safe. The bomb, consisting of a few pounds of military grade C-4, was placed into a large, explosive-proof container on a trailer pulled by the Bomb Squad. It looked like a big pressure cooker on wheels.

Once the Bomb Squad left, Deshawn and his grandmother were allowed to return to their home. John had a patrol car remain at the residence while he went to Grady hospital to check on Doctor Higdon and Mutumbo.

He called Simmons at police dispatch and had him call DIA to get the information to Gillam and Lovett. Simmons, of course, had questions that Starling was not ready to answer and stopped him. He ordered security for Doctor Higdon at the hospital. With so many people being targeted, it was hard to know where Mutumbo's cousin would strike next or try and finish what he started.

When Starling got to the hospital, he immediately went to the Emergency Room where he found Mutumbo. He had a large bandage over his nose and his eyes were swollen.

"It's broken, isn't it?" John asked.

"Yes, but I be worried more about Doctor Higdon. He not wake up."

"Do you know where his doctor is or maybe a nurse who is treating him?"

"No, the doctor be very busy. I just wait."

"Okay, I understand. I'm going to find a doctor or someone who can give me some information." John saw a uniformed officer outside one of the treatment rooms. "Is that where Doctor Higdon is?"

"Yes. he stand at room for about ten minutes. Will not let me see Doctor Higdon."

"I ordered the security, but I'll tell him you can go in with the treating doctor's approval. By the way, your cousin went after the other boy, then tried to blow me up. Put a bomb under my car."

"And you live. I be impressed."

"Thank you," John said, a little surprised. "Me too."

John went in search of the Emergency Room doctor treating Doctor Higdon. He found a nurse who directed him to an office where he located him. He introduced himself as well as showing his identification. He asked about Doctor Higdon.

"I'm afraid he is in a coma right now. There is a blood clot pressing on an artery that we need to be very careful with."

"Are you going to do surgery?" John asked.

"It's too risky right now, we are going to start him on a blood thinner first and hope it helps. We'll leave him here in the Emergency Room for monitoring. We don't want to move him."

"His assistant is also here; can he see him? I don't think he's going anywhere until he does. Maybe not even then."

"What can you tell me about the police guard on him?"

"It's for his protection. That's all I can say about that right now."

"There's been so much happening here, the shootout and all. Are our patients and staff safe?" Doctor Menzell asked.

"Yes, of course," John said, hoping he was right.

"Let's go check on the good doctor."

John went and got Mutumbo, meeting the doctor at the room entrance. Starling showed his identification to the officer before they entered.

Doctor Higdon was on an inhalation machine, an IV in his arm, and a bandage around his head.

Mutumbo took Doctor Higdon's hand, got on his knees beside the bed, and silently prayed.

CHAPTER 52

Mr. Williams received the call from headquarters about a location which was about forty miles outside of Atlanta, in Paulding County. From time to time, there were a few citizens who called into the Sheriff's Office to complain about dancing lights, strange aircraft, and possible UFO's.

Most of these sightings would take place in one general area, but no one ever saw them land or came across them on the ground. The reports were dismissed, attributed to too much alcohol, drugs, regular aircraft, or false reports to generate publicity or notoriety.

A cross check as suggested by Gillam showed that a small, residential, private airfield was purchasing avgas near that same area in Paulding County. However; they were receiving way too much for just a plane or two. The avgas they received could be used in both airplanes and helicopters.

A check on the property revealed that it was privately owned, and was about four-hundred acres, surrounded by trees. Satellite images showed a large house and a large barn, but no aircraft. Later images showed a larger building having been built near the barn, but still no aircraft. A small field which could double as a landing strip could be seen in the second image. All the images had been sent to Mr. Williams who showed them to the group.

"The aircraft could be in the barn, or in the larger building, or gone when the image was taken," Debbie said.

"You think that could be it?" Sam asked.

"It's possible," Mr. Williams said. "We need to get a confirmation on it before we start storming the place."

"And how do you do that?" Connie asked.

"We put our own surveillance on the location," Mr. Williams said, smiling. "Eyes on, drone, satellite, and other ways. Headquarters will keep us informed if there is any movement or other activity.

"So, Big Brother is always watching us," Connie said.

"Of course," Mr. Williams confirmed, "what better way to keep you safe?"

"You mean under control," Sam said. The others just nodded.

It's almost time," Mr. Williams reminded them. "Detective Gillam, if you please." Mr. Williams ushered him into his special room.

Mutumbo's cousin sat cross-legged on the bed in the cheap motel room. In front of him was the case containing the rifle. He was considering going back after the boy. Especially since that detective was gone and Mutumbo and his employer were at the hospital. There was just one policeman and an old lady with a shotgun at the house. He almost laughed.

He never promised Mutumbo he would spare the boy, but it just wouldn't be any fun with him not able to come running to the boy's rescue.

Besides, he had another target today for which he needed to prepare. A much more dangerous target. One he had waited many years to see through his rifle scope. Today would be that day. No need chancing that something would go wrong with the boy. Mutumbo could have him; for now.

The rifle had been cleaned, the scope sighted in for the distance, the bullet specially selected. He should only need one, but had several in reserve. The nest position was previously scouted, escape routes checked, the weather would be perfect.

The wind would be the main thing. Although very mild at street level, it could get tricky that high up and between the buildings, changing rapidly.

This was as he had envisioned it, many, many times. It was hard to believe it was really going to happen in just a short while. It was the main thing that drove him. When it was over, how would he feel? He hadn't thought about a future after the deed. To him, it really didn't matter after that.

He closed the case, got up and took a shower, dressed, then headed out to the now black Chevy Impala.

The DIA headquarters contacted Mr. Williams, letting him know there was some activity at the property in Paulding County. No one had come or gone down the mile long drive, however; the large building next to the barn had a retractable roof and a helicopter flew out of it about five minutes ago, apparently headed for Atlanta; occupants unknown. They wanted to know if they needed to take any action.

Mr. Williams relayed that no action was to be taken at this time, but to continue to monitor the location and the helicopter.

Mr. Williams told the group they most likely found the right location and gave a thumbs up to Detective Gillam. "Good job. I think we could make room for another Agent Gillam if you had a mind to."

"I don't think they could handle it," Larry said.

"I think the three of us could take charge of that place in no time," Brenda said.

"See what I mean," Larry said, "One is enough."

CHAPTER 53

A couple of uniform officers were at the hospital to talk with Mutumbo about the vehicle assault. An initial report needed to be made, both with them and with a Fulton County unit, who was on the way. He was not in the mood to talk with any of them. He excused himself to go to the restroom.

"Give him just a short while," Starling told them. "He's been through a lot."

"We understand," one of the officers stated. "We're still waiting on the Fulton County unit so we'll go get the information we need off the wagon. We saw it out in the Emergency Room parking lot. The driver's window is broken, so we won't need a key. We'll be back shortly, just have Mr. Mutumbo wait for us here."

The officers went out to the parking lot and returned immediately.

"It's gone, detective. I think he took off in it," one of the officers reported. "Do you know where he might have gone?"

"No, I'm afraid not," John lied. "And he doesn't have a cell phone. Maybe he went back to the Medical Examiner's Office. He had blood all over his shirt from the broken nose. He may have gone to change. I'd check there."

The officers left, hurrying out to their patrol car.

John hated to lie, especially to his own guys, but then again, it's possible Mutumbo went to change, and he really didn't know, for sure, where he was. He was glad he didn't lie.

Everyone was getting ready to leave the safehouse to go to Doctor Muhammad's office when Mr. Williams made a request.

"Miss Debbie, I have a favor to ask, please."

"Sure, Mr. Williams, what may I do for you?"

"I don't have anyone to stay and monitor the communications with headquarters if they were to call or send information here. It's not good to leave the station unattended. I was wondering if you would stay and do that for me?"

Debbie looked at Sam with questioning eyes.

"I think that would be a great idea," Sam said, "She is great with communications."

Debbie gave Sam a different look; one not very nice.

"It would really mean a lot to me, otherwise, I would have to stay," Mr. Williams told the white lie.

"Okay, I'll stay. But don't think for a minute I don't know what you're doing. I'm not that pregnant."

"You're pregnant enough," Sam said.

"And Miss Connie, would you stay with her? It's really a security thing. See, neither one of you is DIA and I can't leave one person here alone that's not DIA. It's strictly against protocol. Not that I don't trust either of you, I could get in a lot of trouble if I don't follow the rules."

Connie looked at Larry and he nodded his head and smiled.

She put her bag down. "You could have saved some time by just telling us who wasn't going instead of coming up with a lame excuse."

"I didn't think it was lame at all. I thought it was a good excuse." Larry said.

"It was probably your idea," Connie said.

Larry smiled.

"It was your idea," Connie exclaimed.

"It was mine, "Mr. Williams confessed, "but it garnered the desired results. Now we have plenty of room in one car."

"Oh, brother," Sam said.

Mr. Williams went back into his special room and exited with a tray. It held the .45 Larry had given up and Sam's 9mm and his .38 ankle gun.

"Now I think we're ready," he said.

CHAPTER 54

Mutumbo's cousin took off the backpack which contained a hat and jacket to match the building color, water, a sandwich, and an apple. He placed it next to the case with the rifle parts. He was prepared to stay for a while.

Once, he set up on a target and waited nearly twenty hours to get just the right shot. It almost didn't happen because he was so drained and dehydrated. His vision was affected, his hand trembled, yet somehow, he made the shot. He learned.

He thought of his brother, how scared he must have been, knowing that he was about to take not just his own life, but those of many innocent people, and he couldn't do anything about it.

Now, he was about to kill the person responsible, and they wouldn't even see it coming. It would be over in a split second. No anticipation, no fear, no hope. It didn't seem fair.

He was having second thoughts about his methods when he heard a helicopter echoing off the buildings. It was heading for a landing on the rooftop helipad of the high-rise not far from him.

He watched it land, the rotors coming to stop before several people exited. It was Doctor Muhammad, Doctor Greyson, and two other people unknown to him. They were met by several people who came from the building and escorted the other two off after shaking hands with Doctor Muhammad and Dr. Greyson.

He brought up the unattached scope. Looking at them as they talked on the roof, slowly making their way to the building, oblivious that they were being watched, much less that death would soon be coming their way.

"Thank you, Mr. Williams," Sam said, as they traveled to downtown Atlanta. "I knew she wouldn't stay behind if I asked her."

"Same here," Larry said. "I think both girls are safer there."

"No problem," Mr. Williams stated, "never let it be said that I put a woman and her child, born or unborn, in danger."

His phone rang.

After a short conversation, Mr. Williams reported that the helicopter had landed and several people went into the high-rise, including Doctor Muhammad.

"Good," Larry said. "We know he's there. Let's hope he stays there."

"We now have eyes on him that will tell us if he leaves," Mr. Williams stated.

"I can't wait to see that bastard again," Gillam stated.

"But as we discussed," Mr. Williams reminded him, "you

will not engage him directly."

"I understand," Larry said.

"I'm glad you understand, detective, but I want assurances that you will not assault him."

"I will not assault him, unless he gives me a reason to do so."

"I guess that's the best I can hope for at this point," Mr. Williams stated.

"You're lucky to get that," Brenda added.

"Are we there yet?" Sam asked, breaking up the tension for a brief moment.

Everyone chuckled.

Mutumbo knew his cousin would have checked out several areas to operate from which would give him the best vantage point. He would have done the same, but he didn't have time to check them all. He needed some luck on his side.

He drove the Medical Examiners wagon downtown to the area he knew would be within the target area, looking for buildings which would have the line of sight, elevation, and give the best view possible. Distance was not a huge factor, but he believed within a half mile. That took up a lot of real estate and a bunch of buildings.

Mutumbo didn't know how much time he had, but he was sure it wouldn't be much. His cousin was patient, but if the shot presented itself, he would take it, and be gone.

Mutumbo questioned the reasons why he wanted to stop him in the first place. Why not just let him take out this bad man? Then he would leave and that would be the end of it.

Did he think by stopping him, he would somehow be saving his soul? Did he want to stop him because of Doctor Higdon? Or for his own reasons; reasons that went back many years.

Whatever the reason, Mutumbo knew that stopping his cousin was the right thing to do. Whether he would be able to do it in time was becoming more of the question.

Mr. Williams pulled the car into the pay-to-park lot across the street from the high-rise. When he got out, he paid the fee at the control box, returning to the group.

"Okay gang, are you ready to do this? Let's go see the wizard," he said.

"I've got one here who needs a brain," Brenda said, pointing at Larry."

"I think we all need one at this point" Sam said.

They entered the building and went over to the familiar bank of elevators. They were stopped by the security guards.

"We have an appointment with Doctor Muhammad," Mr. Williams stated.

The guard scanned his books. "There's no appointments

listed for today," he said. He looked at the four standing in front of him and seemed to look closer at Larry and Brenda. "Do I know you?" he asked.

"I don't know, do you?" Larry stated.

The guard shook his head. "Sorry, I see a lot of faces and they all seem to run together. There's nothing here and we have not been informed of any changes. I'll call and check with his receptionist."

"We'd rather you not do that. We have an appointment, but he doesn't know about it." Brenda said.

"Huh," the security guard looked completely dumbfounded, which was very easy for him to do.

Mr. Williams showed his government badge and identification as did Brenda. Gillam and Sam showed their Atlanta Police Detective badges and identification.

Mr. Williams extended an arm and with his hand, twirled one finger around. Four DIA agents swarmed to him. "Keep these gentlemen busy, please. No calls or radios."

"It's nice to have friends in strange places," Larry said. "That's just the beginning," Brenda said. She got on her phone. "Cut it," she said.

Mr. Williams nodded and one of the DIA agents flipped the switch for the elevators and the doors opened.

He motioned to two of the agents to join them. "I want you to secure the pilot and the helicopter and anyone who comes to the helipad."

"Will do," they said.

The elevator took off for the top floors.

"What about the cameras," Larry asked.

Brenda smiled. "Taken care of."

"Good." Larry made one last preparation.

They arrived at the floor of Doctor Omar Muhammad.

CHAPTER 55

Mutumbo knew he was out there. He knew today was the day. He drove around block after block, trying to locate his cousin's car or see an ideal location to set up the sniper's nest.

He wasn't going to be able to do it from the wagon, he needed to get some elevation. There were a few buildings taller than the office high-rise and many more which would be suitable to set up in, either from a window or the roof. Mutumbo was just going to have to guess.

He parked, going to one of the largest buildings. He was in luck. This one had an observation area he could get to.

He went up and out to the area which had a fence around the edge so no one would accidently fall or intentionally jump.

The target high-rise could be seen, helicopter on the roof. He strained to see if there was anyone on the roofs of other buildings, or windows open on top floors. He knew he would be hard to pick out. He cupped his hands over his eyes, but he still didn't see anything. He waited, hoping some movement would catch his eye. His area of vision limited, it was going to take a miracle. But Mutumbo believed in miracles. He needed a couple of them today. One to find his cousin and one for Doctor Higdon.

As Mutumbo continued to look, he said silent prayers. He

prayed that Doctor Higdon would recover, be able to return to work soon, and suffer no ill effects.

He also prayed that he would find his cousin, stop his terrible deeds, and put him on the right path. He wasn't sure either prayer would be answered, but he knew which one he wanted.

He also— Mutumbo's eyes widened. Was that a glimmer of light. A reflection where no reflection should be. It could have been the Sun's reflection off a plastic water bottle, or it could have been a piece of paper caught up in the swirls of wind. There were a million things it could be; he just needed it to be one.

He made a mental note of the building, the location on the roof of that building, then he hurried to the exit. It might take ten minutes to get there. He hoped he still had that long.

Mr. Williams, Larry, Sam, and Brenda stepped out of the elevator as the other DIA agents went up to the roof when the doors closed.

The receptionist, the same one who was there last time, looked surprised when they stepped off the elevator and started walking in her direction. She picked up the phone, but Brenda got to her quickly. This time, there were no words, the receptionist put the phone down slowly. Brenda opened the drawer to the woman's desk, removing the elevator key card, and this time, a small can of pepper spray.

"Really," Brenda laughed, "Where is he?"

"Who?" The receptionist played dumb.

Brenda just looked at her. It was very intimidating.

"He's in his office with Doctor Greyson."

"You sit here, don't even think about leaving, and don't touch that phone."

"Yes, ma'am."

Brenda stared at her.

"I mean, no ma'am."

They went to the big oak doors which went to the office of Doctor Omar Muhammad, and opened them.

It took Mutumbo a long time to get to the street floor of the building he had been in. There were too many stops along the way. The stairs would not have been any better of an option.

He had to orientate himself to the building he just exited and the target building. Now other buildings blocked his way. It looked so different at this level and much further away. He ran.

Doctor Muhammad was sitting at his desk. Doctor Greyson sat on the couch. Both stood when the four entered the office.

"What is this?" Muhammad demanded.

"Doctor Omar Muhammad, I'm Agent Gillam, DIA.

We're taking you into protective custody. There's a man out there planning to kill you. Possibly today."

"That's ridiculous," he said. "I can take care of myself. Get out of my office. Now."

"That's not going to happen," Mr. Williams said.

"Doctor Greyson, would you call security and get these people out," Doctor Muhammad requested.

"Your security is a little tied up," Mr. Williams explained. "If we can get to you, so can he. You are not under arrest, this is for your safety. Now, stop complaining and please come with us."

Doctor Muhammad reached over to his desk and pressed a button.

"I hope that was your lawyer on speed dial," Brenda stated. "I have a court order here for you to comply. Your lawyer will tell you to do the same."

"I'm not going anywhere. Detective Gillam, are you ready to help me again?" Doctor Muhammad quickly said the phrase he had repeated the last time they had met. The one that turned him into an obeying zombie.

Gillam stood there, motionless.

"Detective Larry Gillam, I'm sorry to do this, but shoot your friends. Now"

Mutumbo's cousin had the rifle together and was

adjusting the focus. When it cleared, he saw the target building, the office, and his target. However, he saw a lot more than that.

There were a number of others in the office; three men and a woman. He didn't recognize any of them, however, they looked like cops.

Even as good a shape as Mutumbo was in, he was a little winded when he got to the entrance of the building, having run flat out. He knew he would never make it up all those stairs. The elevator was the only choice. It didn't have an express and each stop was agony. He stood at the door, allowing people to get off, but not allowing anyone to get in. He made more than a few people angry.

Finally, he was alone in the elevator. People arriving at their stops or getting off because he scared them. It got to the top floor and he searched around until he found the exit to the stairwell which also had a sign for roof access.

Mutumbo's cousin looked through the telescopic lens, curious as to what was going on in that office. It looked like an argument.

He took the rifle off the ledge perch and loaded one special bullet into the chamber. Now he was ready to take the shot when it presented itself.

He set the rifle on the steady perch once more, aimed through the scope, placing the crosshairs on his target, and waited.

Gillam stared at Doctor Muhammad.

"Shoot them, I said." He pointed at the other three. "Shoot them right now."

Gillam turned, facing the other three. He took the .45 automatic out of his waistband in the back of his pants, pointing it down. "Kill, kill, kill," he said. Then he turned and almost bent over and started laughing. "Is that what you said because I can't hear a thing with these earplugs in?" He said way too loud.

"Oops," Mr. Williams said.

Just then, a secret panel opened at the side wall and two men with guns stepped through. With his gun already out, Gillam was able to get the first shot off, hitting one man in the leg. A bullet whizzed by his ear so close, he could feel the heat.

Mr. Williams quickly drew and fired, hitting the man Gillam shot, putting him down for good.

Doctor Muhammad and Doctor Greyson took cover behind his desk.

The second man fired wildly at Sam and Brenda as he ran for cover behind the globe. He didn't make it. Brenda, never flinching, made her one and only shot count.

Sam went over and looked at the men. They were the

same ones he had arrested and gone to Grand Jury on. They were the brothers of Muhammad.

"Get up," Sam said, "Get over here."

Muhammad and Greyson stood and came around to the front of the desk.

"What's going on," Sam asked. "I want the truth, all of it."

"I want an attorney," Greyson demanded.

"So did they," Sam said, pointing at the men on the floor.

Mutumbo's cousin was so enthralled by what was going on in the office, he didn't see Mutumbo come out on the roof.

"Ezekiel, put rifle down," Mutumbo shouted.

"That is no longer my name. Do not call me that."

"It be only name I know. It be only name your mother give you. You must not do this bad thing."

"You are wrong. I must. My brother calls out to me to do this. It is him who begs for justice."

"Your brother be dead. I'm sorry, he no longer speaks."

"He speaks to me all the time, cousin. Open your ears, maybe he will speak to you."

"The dead stay dead. The living will join them soon enough, but there be good and bad places to be. Do you not want to be in God's hands?"

"God has washed his hands of me, cousin. I bring death

and it is a good thing. I know what my fate is and I except it. Go now, let me do my work." Ezekiel looked back through the scope, getting a bead on his target.

Mutumbo pulled 'Betsy' from behind his back, pointing it at Ezekiel. "I wish you to stop now. Put rifle down."

Ezekiel took a quick peek at Jacob. "Are you sure you can shoot someone now, especially your own family?" Ezekiel asked. "Isn't that the same thing that you were warning me about? Don't go and get yourself sent to Hell."

Jacob lowered the gun.

"I be forgiven, we both be forgiven. Please put rifle down. Come with me."

"I'm sorry, Jacob. I can see my target and I must listen to my brother." He took a deep breath, letting most of it out as he tightened the pressure on the trigger.

"Do not do this," Mutumbo begged. He brought the gun up once again.

"Yes, brother," Ezekiel was saying. "You can sleep without fear again. I am waiting for your word."

"Now, you are under arrest," Mr. Williams told Muhammad.

"And as for you, Doctor Greyson, you—

There was just the slightest sound of glass tinkling and Doctor Greyson jerked just a touch, gave a funny look as blood started to run down her forehead and her nose from a small hole that suddenly appeared just below her hairline. She fell to her knees, arms at her side and then crumpled on the floor.

There was a look of surprise from everyone, then they quickly took cover, away from the window.

Mutumbo was surprised not just by the loud report, but by the kick of the handgun. He looked to see the surprise on Ezekiel's face.

"You shot me, cousin, you really shot me." Ezekiel stated.

He had a small bit of blood coming from where the bullet creased his leg.

"I be glad I not kill you, cousin." Jacob said.

"Me too. You are not a good shot, which is a good thing for me."

"Or maybe I be better shot than to believe. So, I would not try me again. It be time for you to go."

"Yes, but I want you to have this, it may explain some things," Ezekiel said, handing him a large envelope from the rifle case. "Not everything is as it seems." He took the rifle apart, closed the case, and left the roof.

Mutumbo sat down where his cousin had sat. Ezekiel had forgotten to take his back pack. Jacob opened it and took out the apple. He wondered if he would ever see him again.

When the coast appeared to be clear, Mr. Williams went over to Doctor Muhammad and put handcuffs on him.

"I don't want a lawyer," the doctor stated. "I'll tell you anything you want to know. It was all her." Nodding at the body of Doctor Greyson. "I just did the plastic surgery's. She did all the mind stuff. I worked for her."

For over an hour, Doctor Muhammad continued to blabber, telling everything he knew. He admitted to financing Doctor Greyson's experiments, the helicopter and the hidden property in Paulding County was hers, and so much more.

He told how Detective Gillam had been chosen for an experiment to infiltrate the Atlanta Police Department after the news reports of his incident. They thought he might be a good candidate, but were unaware just how strong he was. The dossier given to Jacob verified the information about Doctor Greyson.

He even told how after his brothers were arrested, they had made it a game with a cash prize for Lovett's head; bringing in mercenaries, death squads, and others from terrorist based countries to try and win the prize. Gillam was a secondary target.

With them dead, it was no longer viable and information was quickly disseminated by the DIA that there was never a prize and no money. They reported that the whole time it was a cover operation by the CIA to bring and kill terrorist on US soil for their own purpose.

Giving it a week to settle down, check the chatter, and just to be safe, it appeared everyone could go home once again.

CHAPTER 56

Mutumbo was at Doctor Higdon's side when he woke. A little hoarse and sore from the feeding tube, but in good spirits. He wanted an update about what he had missed, then he wanted some real food.

Mutumbo gave thanks for answered prayers.

Detective John Starling finally had that dinner alone with Dorothy. He had breakfast at her place too.

He had some serious thoughts to share with her and he received her support for whatever direction he wanted to go. But she thought that his plans were wonderful and very noble. She told him it was maybe good for him.

John was making arrangements to take his retirement and open a boy's camp. Someplace where boys could go to be shown that they have alternatives. Get them away from the influences of gangs, crime, drugs, and hopelessness. To give them a positive push in their young lives and role models to really look up to.

He had talked with Detective Gillam and Lovett and they were behind it all the way and would be happy to help.

In fact, Gillam had talked with his ex, Agent Brenda

Gillam of the DIA, and as it turned out, after she spoke with her bosses, and pushing as she was known to do, a certain piece of property in Paulding County, which had been confiscated recently, might make the perfect place. But there was a cost. The government couldn't just give the property away. So, it was leased for a dollar a year. Win-win.

With Detective John Starling retiring, there was an opening in the Homicide Squad. There was already one of the detectives from the squad on suspension, so they needed someone to fill the void quickly.

An up and coming young detective by the name of Caution Murphy was placed on the Homicide Squad. She had shown an uncanny ability to solve some of the hardest cases in the Larceny Squad and the brass wanted to give her a chance.

Sometimes referred to as 'strange' or 'eccentric', she mostly kept to herself. Sometimes, she was seen talking to inanimate objects or to herself.

And the girl had money. Inheriting a bundle, including her own building with a penthouse. She never talked about it though.

CHAPTER 57

Now with an opening in Larceny, Detective Lovett was considering the move. He was sure that Debbie would love for him to get the safer assignment with better hours. It was something he had talked with Gillam about.

With the opening available for only a limited time, he had made the decision. He knew what he had to do. His family came first. But wasn't Larry part of his family? He had been with him a long time. They had saved each other's skin many times.

How was Larry going to feel? Let down, of course. Abandoned? Disappointed?

He had to get over this. Larry was his partner, not his wife. Debbie was having a baby. He was going to be a father. It wasn't fair to Debbie to have to worry so much. It could even affect the pregnancy.

Larry was just going to have to make the best of it. Maybe he would get excited about training a new guy. He enjoyed that part of the job almost as much as putting the bad guys away.

Sam would try to let him know the decision was hard, let him down easy. This wasn't going to be pretty. Sam took a deep breath and walked into the Narcotics Squad.

"There's my old partner," Larry said. He was holding several boxes. "I got these to help you move." There was a big smile on his face.

"Thanks," Sam said.

"Hey, don't look so glum, chum. It's going to be great. I hear they get the best doughnuts down there." The Larceny Squad was two floors down.

"They gave me Tuesdays and Wednesdays off," Sam said "It's like I'm starting all over."

"Hey, you got the day shift. What more do you want?" Larry said. "Besides no one shooting at you, trying to tear your head off, or putting a pig sticker in your ribs."

"Yeah, there's that," Sam said, with very little enthusiasm.

"Well, let's get you packed. I'll help you move," Larry offered. "I haven't been down there in years. Let's go get you set up."

"You haven't been down there in years?" Sam repeated.

"Well, I really didn't know anyone down there. Now, I know you. I'll try to get down there once in a while."

Sam was glad Larry was putting on such a brave face and trying to help him ease into his new assignment. He just wished that Larry wasn't so brave.

"Hey, Gillam, the Chief wants to see you," one of the squad members shouted.

"Okay. I'll get right there. Let me just help my old

partner to his new home."

Speaking of a new home; when Sam and Debbie arrived at their house, they found it completely renovated to include a beautiful nursery, courtesy of the DIA.

Gillam was really happy for Lovett, but he wasn't really happy for himself. He lost the best partner he ever had. He hoped the friendship wouldn't suffer. He would make a note of ball games and other events they could get together for.

He had talked with Debbie and she asked him to go along with the reassignment. She was so worried about him getting hurt or worse. She knew it wasn't like her to be that worried, but the pregnancy could be the reason. Maybe after the baby was born, she would feel different. He doubted it.

After helping Sam, Gillam went to the Chief's office and the secretary showed him in.

"Have a seat, Detective Gillam. You've been through a lot lately, haven't you? Lost your gun and badge too, I hear."

"Yes, sir. Thank you for backing me on things. I think I'm okay now. No more problems."

"Well, that's one of the things I want to talk with you about."

"Sir?"

"You're fired."

"What?" Gillam said, almost coming out of his chair.

"You're no longer a Sergeant in the Narcotics Squad."

"I'm not?" Larry was about to say something bad.

"No," the Chief said. "You're the new Lieutenant of the Narcotics Squad."

"Oh, God," Larry said, sitting heavily back down in the chair, "what have I gotten myself into now?"

"Congratulations," the Chief said, handing him his shiny, new, lieutenant's badge. "I guess you'll be wanting a new gun too?"

That weekend, Larry and Connie made it to the North Georgia Mountains. They both needed the mental rest, the solitude, and each other.

Leaving from the Port of Savannah, a cargo ship headed out to sea. Onboard was a man with a strange name. Also onboard was a large container housing a very unique car belonging to the man. He was on a quest.

THANK YOU

I want to thank everyone for reading my detective series. I hope you enjoyed it. Independent authors rely heavily upon reviews and word-of-mouth to reach new readers. If you have a moment to spare, please leave a review on your preferred site. Honest reviews, short or long, are greatly appreciated.

Amazon.com/author/williamngilmore

Goodreads.com/author/show/17055576.William_N_Gilmore

ABOUT THE AUTHOR

William N. Gilmore is a Retired Atlanta Police Detective with nearly 27 years on the force to include 15 years working on the Narcotics Squad. He is also a Vietnam era veteran, serving 7 years with the U. S. Army as a Military Policeman, serving a total of four years in Atlanta at Ft. McPherson, GA. He is a member of the Paulding County Writers' Guild. He enjoys metal detecting for Civil War items, gold panning, photography, and his family. He lives in Hiram, GA with his lovely wife, Esther.

www.williamngilmore.wordpress.com